Holly

Satin

Boots

By Holly Bargo

HEN HOUSE PUBLISHING
Springfield, Ohio USA
https://www.henhousepublishing.com

Acknowledgments

First and foremost, I thank my husband who has learned that the voices in my head really do need to come out and play. Understanding isn't necessary; but I am grateful for the acceptance.

As always, thanks go to my editor, Cindy Draughon, whose keen eye and insight pick out those inconsistencies, discrepancies, and typos that would otherwise result in a disreputable mess of a manuscript.

Last, but not least, I deeply appreciate those who read and enjoy my stories. I hope this one entertains you and leaves you wanting more.

Table of Contents

Angels High

A woman who makes her living by winning at a man's game learns to expect trouble, especially when the stakes are high. But when trouble finds her this time, Angelica Durant gets more than she bargained for.

Twisting the end of his luxurious mustache, Albert Derringer looked at the woman who took a newly vacated seat at the table. She'd been sitting nearby, watching the play for the last hour. Setting both hands on the table, he leaned forward and said, "Ma'am, women ain't allowed to gamble here."

The woman leaned forward, displaying a hint of décolletage, just enough to pique a man's interest and distract his thoughts, and said, "Show me where that's written and I'll leave."

Albert couldn't because the establishment had no such written code of conduct and admittance. The woman's lips curled in a tiny smile of triumph. She opened her reticule and pulled out the money for her stake in the game. The four other men at the table looked at the gold coins with greedy interest.

"Al, if she's got the money, let her play," Harold Everhart said as he rubbed his palms together. "We'll be happy to win her money."

"I like the looks of her money and her face," Chester MacAllister remarked with a curt nod. "Better'n looking at your ugly mugs, boys."

Good-natured laughter followed his comment.

"Deal the lady in," Jesse Cordoba said, his voice cool and haughty as befitted the son of a Spanish hidalgo and a Boston society debutante.

The fourth player, expression concealed behind a bushy black beard stained with tobacco and other substances, grunted and nodded, which the others inferred as assent.

With a sigh meant to convey unwilling obedience to the gamblers' wishes, the dealer picked up a deck of cards.

"If you don't mind," the woman said as she withdrew a brand new deck of cards from her handbag, "please use these. I'd hate to soil my new gloves on those filthy cards."

Not one man there could argue that the cards they had been playing with were dirty. They looked at her pristine white gloves and sighed with resignation.

"How do we know them cards ain't marked?" Harold inquired with beady-eyed suspicion.

Chester snorted at the idea that a woman, even one who cheated, could match wits and card playing skills with them.

Reaching across the table, she handed Harold the small cardboard box. In a soft southern drawl that hinted at beignets, strong coffee, and sweet spices from far off lands across the sea, she replied, "It hasn't even been opened, sir. Please, do check it to verify. I have neither the desire nor the inclination to be dishonest with you fine gentlemen."

Harold looked over the box, noting that the paper wrapper had not been disturbed. With a nod, he handed it to Jesse who examined it and passed it around the table until it returned to the woman who handed it to the dealer. Albert looked it over and, since the other players did not object to using the lady's deck of cards, found nothing for complaint. He shrugged his shoulders and, with deft efficiency, broke the seal, unwrapped the fresh deck, and shuffled the cards.

Chester leaned toward the woman to get a closer peek down her bodice and asked, "And what's your name, pretty lady?"

The woman toyed with a shining curl of mink colored hair that dangled near her collarbone and answered, "Angelica Durand. And might I know your name, sir?"

The men introduced themselves in turn. Angelica shook hands with all of them, her gloved fingers touching their bare skin. Both Chester and the full-bearded man everyone called "Goose" looked pained when she leaned across the table to complete the introductions. She ignored the movement of their arms when they lowered their hands beneath the table and shifted awkwardly in their seats to adjust themselves.

Jesse Cordoba's black eyes flickered a glittering look at her that she could not yet interpret, but which seemed to hold a challenge. Angelica's slow blink answered it with her own unspoken challenge.

"Do you know the game, ma'am?" Albert asked as he dealt the cards.

"Poker, five card stud," she replied with a small smile. "Am I correct?"

"Yes, ma'am. I assume you've played before?"

"Once or twice."

The five men nodded, each thinking to himself that he'd quit the table that night a good deal richer than when he entered the game. Angelica pulled off her gloves and laid them in her lap. Every man at the table and some beyond focused on the reveal of pale skin. None thought to point out the discrepancy between her statement of not wanting to soil her gloves and her obvious intention to play cards without them.

As the hand played out and Harold called, those who hadn't folded revealed their cards. Groans echoed around the table when the lady showed a full house made of three queens and two tens.

"I believe my hand beats yours, sir," she said in a sweet tone as Goose showed his full house: two kings and three eights.

Albert gathered the cards, shuffled, and dealt again. The lady folded on the second hand, lost the third, and won the fourth, fifth, and sixth hands. Then Harold won the next three hands. As he prepared to discard a card, Angelica pulled out a short, sharp knife and aimed it at the back of his left hand.

"Set your cards down, sir," she ordered, every syllable dripping icy contempt. "I don't hold with cheaters."

"You dare call me a cheater, you bitch?" Harold snarled.

Without retreating or flinching, Angelica said, "Mr. Derringer, please check his left sleeve. He has a card hidden up there."

"You lie!" Harold shouted. His face reddened and sweat beaded on his forehead and upper lip.

The ominous click of a hammer commanded everyone's attention. Jesse aimed a shiny, pearl handled pistol at him. No one had seen him draw it. But then, no one had seen that nasty little knife either until the woman drew it from her sleeve.

"Allow Albert to examine your sleeve, Harold," Jesse ordered. "If she's wrong, then she leaves the table. If she's right, then your winnings are forfeit and *you* leave the table."

"You got no cause—" Harold protested, but Goose lumbered to his feet. Big hands landed heavily on Harold's shoulders in an unbreakable grip.

Angelica's eyes widened as she realized just how big that man was.

Held immobile by the bearded giant, Harold had no choice but to submit to examination. Albert frowned in disappointment when he pulled an ace from the man's sleeve and held it up for the rest of the players to see. Angelica slid the small knife back up her sleeve and out of sight.

"Get out," the giant grumbled and shoved Harold from the table.

"You're lucky we don't kill you, you cheater," Chester snapped.

"You have sharp eyes, madam," Jesse complimented with a nod of admiration.

She responded with a modest smile and curt nod, but said nothing. Albert divvied up Harold's winnings among the remaining four players and the house, gathered the cards, and re-shuffled the deck. The next several hands passed with Angelica winning more than losing.

Finally, the clock struck midnight. Angelica gathered her winnings and stuffed them into her reticule. She rose to her feet, smiled at the other gamblers, and said, "Thank you, gentlemen, for an excellent game. It's late and I need my beauty rest. Mr. Derringer, you may keep the deck of cards."

"Allow me to escort you to your lodging," Jesse offered as he stood, too.

The others scrambled to their feet, remembering their manners in the presence of a lady. Angelica smiled at him, then turned her attention toward Goose.

"I shall fear no assault with your escort, Mr. Goose. Will you ensure my safety?"

Drawing himself up to his full, imposing height, Goose nodded in assent, although he looked dumbfounded by the request. He gathered his winnings and shoved them deep into the pockets of his dirty trousers.

"Why, thank you, Mr. Goose," she said.

Goose grunted, turning pink with pleasure beneath the whiskers and above that hawk's beak of a nose. Clumsy, as if he'd not had much in the way of practice at being a gentleman, he held out his arm. She lightly placed her gloved hand on his dirty sleeve. She bade the other gamblers a good night, and departed.

Goose kept a wary eye out for anyone who might entertain stupid notions of molesting the pretty woman as he walked her to the boarding house where she told him she had taken a room. The light touch of her gloved hand and the sound of her swishing skirts ignited a combination of feelings he'd not experienced before, but he recognized them as a strange mixture of possessiveness, lust, and protectiveness.

He was grateful she did not chatter at him like many women did, but held her tongue in peaceful, companionable silence. When they arrived at the boarding house, she patted his arm and spoke for the first time since they'd left the poker table.

"Thank you, Mr. Goose. You've been most gracious."

He nodded, shuffled his big, booted feet, and opened his mouth to say something as she turned to leave. To his surprise, he did not want to lose her company.

She must have seen his jaw working beneath the bushy concealment of his beard, because she paused and asked, "Yes, Mr. Goose? You wished to speak to me?"

He was glad the late hour and his whiskers prevented her from seeing his face flush red with embarrassment. After a few more seconds, he finally blurted, "Tomorrow?"

Angelica tilted her head to one side. That lone curl dragged along the creamy skin over her collarbone. Goose felt his body react.

"You mean will I join your game tomorrow?"

"Uh huh," he grunted and shoved his hands into his pockets to keep from grabbing the woman.

"If I'm welcome at the table, I'd be delighted to accept

your kind invitation, Mr. Goose," she replied and patted his arm again.

Goose thought he'd melt into warm goo at the touch. It emboldened him to speak again. "I'll escort you."

Her pretty smile widened with delight and he thought the very stars sparkled in her big brown eyes.

"Why, that's mighty kind of you, sir. You are a true gentleman."

He managed a smile and thought that if she knew what he wanted to do with her and to her, she'd retract that compliment in a heartbeat. However, he felt proud for having beaten out the slick Spanish half-breed in having captured the lady's interest. The bastard had women crawling all over him. Goose was lucky if he could get a whore to accept his money.

So immersed in his thoughts that he did not hear the door close softly behind her, Goose decided that the lady deserved better than the slovenly mountain man who'd provided that night's safe escort, and made plans to buy himself some new clothes, a bath, and a shave.

Angelica dumped her winnings on the bed in her room and tallied the amount, pleased at the sum from that night's work. A few more games like that and she'd have enough to pay back her debt to Cousin Horace, although she was sure he'd continue to blackmail her. Really, it wasn't her fault that he'd been banned from all the best salons and gaming hells in Chicago, Memphis, and St. Louis, even though he blamed his dishonor on her. She had not forced him to cheat, even though she'd taught him how and exposed his perfidy.

Really, was it her fault that Papa taught her everything he knew, giving her the means to make a living that didn't involve lying on her back? Was it her fault that she was good—extremely good—at it? Was it her fault that in trying to teach Horace some of that skill to improve his own game that he'd use it with dishonor?

She shook her head and knew. No, it wasn't her fault. But she had taught him, given him ability where he'd had none before without considering how he might use it. Her so-called betrayal when she revealed his cheating had far-reaching consequences.

"With knowledge comes responsibility," Papa reminded her during their lessons.

Her belly rumbled, protesting its emptiness. She promised to fill it at breakfast the next morning and prepared herself for bed.

Accustomed to functioning on only a few hours of sleep, Angelica rose early and joined the other lodgers for breakfast. As promised, the house provided a substantial meal that stuck to one's ribs like glue. It also sank in one's belly like lead.

"Where might I find a bookstore?" she asked the proprietor.

"In Copperhead Gulch?" the woman asked, eyes wide with surprise. "There ain't no bookstore here, but the general store might have a few to sell."

"Thank you, ma'am," Angelia said and headed out, keeping her handbag tucked tightly against her body. Having spent much of her childhood in such places, she knew better than to leave money in a boarding house room.

As she strolled through town, she noticed other women looking at her, taking note of her fashionable garb and jaunty hat. She knew she looked like a flashy peacock among drab sparrows and wrens, but the fancy outfit was necessary to her profession. No one gambled with a woman who looked indigent. It was difficult enough to insert herself into a game, despite her skill.

Angelica pondered the gamblers with whom she'd played the previous night, recalling their tells. Jesse Cordoba tended to blink more rapidly than usual when he had a winning hand and affect a superior little grin when he hadn't. An old-fashioned gambler, Chester MacAllister's left shoulder drooped ever so slightly when he held a winning hand. Otherwise his expression, gestures, and posture gave nothing away. Goose presented an enigma. He held himself still like a hunter watching prey, preparing for ambush. The full beard concealed his facial expressions. He grunted infrequently, which was more than he spoke. But he seemed to have no guile, no tricks. He played with straightforward honesty, winning with simple pleasure and accepting his losses with good grace.

He played for entertainment, she realized. The other men played for income, as did she.

Angelica smiled to herself as she entered the store and perused the merchandise. She knew Goose desired her. Men did, although she did not consider herself particularly beautiful. Papa had taught her to make the most of her *assets*, as he'd called them.

"A hint intrigues a man more than blatant display," he advised her. "Buttons up the front of a woman's bodice make a man think of little but unbuttoning them to see what's beneath. A single curl along a woman's neck makes a man think of whispering sweet nothings in her ear."

So, she waged a subliminal battle of distraction to give her an extra edge in the profession she inherited from her father, along with the skills that designated her a card sharp.

"Card mechanic," Papa explained with pedantic enthusiasm. "This is not cheating. We don't mark the cards in any way, stuff cards up our sleeves, or use any other underhanded methods to beat our opponents."

Angelica rather liked beating her opponents—almost always men—honestly, with her wits and skill.

"Good morning, Miss Durand." The smooth voice of Jesse Cordoba behind her interrupted her thoughts as she looked over the meager selection of books displayed on a single shelf. "You look lovely today."

Disappointed in the paltry selection of reading material, Angelica looked up at the handsome gambler and gave him a polite smile, an empty smile that meant absolutely nothing. "Why, Mr. Cordoba, it's delightful to make your acquaintance again. What brings you to this fine establishment this beautiful morning?"

He held up a tin of tobacco. "Replenishing my supplies."

She peered at it and recognized the brand. "Ah, my Cousin Horace favors that particular blend."

"Whenever I stay in a location for more than a few weeks, I have it shipped to me from New Orleans," he said.

"New Orleans is a fascinating city. I consider it my home," she replied and reached for a book on the shelf. It was dusty. She glanced at the cover and flipped through the first few pages. She murmured, "Sir Arthur Conan Doyle." She looked at Jesse and asked, "Have you read any of his work?"

"No, I can't say as I have," Jesse admitted, looking haughty and superior, a man who did not sully his mind with such frivolous things as fiction.

She turned that polite, empty smile on him again. "Well, I suppose I'll just have to take a chance." She glanced at the eight other books languishing on the shelf. "I've already read Rudyard Kipling's work. Immensely entertaining."

Jesse accompanied her as she headed toward the counter to pay for the book. He said, "I am surprised at your choice of purchase. You look like the kind of woman to take great interest in ribbons and lace."

Expression turning frosty, she turned toward him and asked, "Do I look like I need further embellishment, sir?"

The corners of the man's mouth curled upward a tiny bit as he leaned toward her and whispered into her ear, "You are quite aware that your beauty needs no improvement, madam. I should like to see it unfettered by cloth."

Cheeks flushing at his effrontery, Angelica leaned away from him. "Sir, you are impertinent. You should not say such things to me."

He chuckled, a dark, sensual sound. "Madam, you cannot expect me to think you untouched. You sat in a saloon for over an hour and watched our game before summoning the brass courage to join us. You're no delicate lady."

Angelica's expression congealed into icy disdain. "Nor am I a prostitute."

He chuckled again and ran a finger down her cheek before she could avoid the touch. "Oh, I'm sure you don't charge for it and I know I never pay for it."

Angelica's hand whipped out and slapped him in offense. "Sir! You are insulting."

A shadow loomed over them and a heavy hand settled over Jesse's right shoulder.

"Don't insult the lady," a baritone voice growled.

Jesse looked up and blinked at the startling transformation of the mountain man whose beard had been trimmed close to his skin, his hair cropped close to his head, and his dirty clothes swapped out for clean, if plain, attire. He recovered from his surprise almost instantly and retorted, "Goose, the woman's a card sharp, not a lady."

Angelica's eyes narrowed in righteous outrage. "Are you accusing me of cheating?"

Jesse's eyes narrowed in response. "Since I'm a gentleman, I would not dream of leveling such an accusation at you." Then his expression eased, turned sensual. "However, I *could* be persuaded to regard you in a most favorable light."

Seething, Angelica clenched her jaw and breathed through her nose. After taking a moment to compose herself, she snapped, "Good day, sir."

Goose's firm grip held Jesse in place while she walked to the counter to finish her transaction.

"That wasn't nice, Jesse," Goose growled.

"That woman played us all like a fiddle last night," Jesse sneered. "I've only seen one other person play like that and she looks just like that thieving bastard."

Goose could not deny that the woman had indeed played with uncommon skill. Still ... "She didn't cheat, Jesse. In fact, she showed up Harold as a cheater. I didn't catch him, nor did you, Chester, or Albert. I'd say we owe her a debt, else Harold would've fleeced us."

Jesse snorted, unappeased.

"You're just sore 'cause you were outplayed by a woman," Goose accused.

"No woman beats me at cards," the man growled.

Goose forbore to point out that, indeed, one had.

"I'll get mine back," the gambler added under his breath as he watched Angelica Durand sashay out the door, fancy skirts swaying like a lure. Goose looked, too, unable to tear his eyes away from her.

"Fancy the woman, do you?" Jesse murmured, raising an eyebrow as he took in the unfamiliar sight of the mountain man bereft of the bushy beard, soiled buckskins, and patched, dirty shirt. "Got yourself all clean and gussied up for her. She'll not waste her time on the likes of you."

Goose shrugged, though his cheeks heated with embarrassment beneath the close-trimmed beard. He saw no point in denying the accusation and merely retorted, "At least I didn't insult her."

Jesse's full lips pressed into a thin line of anger. Goose felt a tingle of satisfaction at having drawn blood with that verbal jab.

"See you tonight," he said and left the slick gambler behind.

Emerging from the store's dim interior, Goose blinked at the sudden brightness of the sunshine even as he looked down the street to catch a glimpse of those dark red skirts that made a man think carnal thoughts. He saw nothing and decided that she'd probably stepped into one of the other establishments in the town's small commercial area. He considered her limited options: two restaurants, a doctor's office, post office, saloons, sheriff's office, jail, and two churches, one for the Catholics and the other for everyone else. Unlike some of the other towns he had visited, this one had been founded and laid out by Spanish immigrants and their descendants according to the edicts created by some king of Spain. The distinguishing feature was the central plaza where townsfolk held holiday festivals, political rallies, and other community events.

The big iron bell in the Catholic church's steeple rang the hour as it did every single day, informing all within hearing range of the time. Goose paused to listen to the deep, sonorous sound and thought that he would always associate the ringing of the bells with the concept of civilization. He sighed. As attractive as he found the lady gambler, he could not envision her living in his crude, tiny cabin hidden in the mountains. He sighed again and acknowledged that Jesse was probably right: she'd never look twice at a big lout like him.

The rich glow of dark red fabric caught his eye. *Ah, there she is!* Despite Goose's certainty that Angelica would not waste time on him, enthusiasm, hope, and desire resurged. He headed toward the post office.

"Miss Durand!" he hailed.

Glossy dark curls gleamed beneath the jaunty hat with its dashing embellishment of ivory netting and short, golden feathers. The narrow sleeves of her dress outlined slender arms and the tightly fitting bodice showcased a shapely figure. She turned around and, eyes widening in surprise, responded with a friendly smile.

"Why, Mr. Goose, how lovely to meet you again this morning," she called to him and extended her hand. The other held the book she purchased. Her reticule dangled from that wrist. Goose's sharp eyes noted that the fabric pouch appeared to have reduced somewhat in volume.

Reaching her, he took her gloved hand in his. He turned her hand over and bent over it, bringing the back of her knuckles to his lips for a courtly peck. His senses swirled as the scent of whatever fragrance she'd dabbed on the inside of her wrists wafted up his nose and scrambled his brain. Straightening, he tucked her hand into the crook of his elbow.

"I'll escort you wherever you'd like to go, ma'am," he blurted. "Make sure you're safe."

She blinked and smiled again, although he saw some confusion in her pretty brown eyes. He felt the need to elaborate.

"Copperhead Gulch is a rough town, 'specially for a pretty lady. Lotsa men here what won't care none if you ain't interested in their attention."

Her expression warmed and she gave his arm a little squeeze that made his heartbeat quicken.

"Then I shall be glad of, and honored by, your escort, Mr. Goose."

Quelling the urge to whoop with triumph, he grinned and said, "It's just Goose, ma'am."

She took a step and he fell into stride beside her, taking pride in having such an attractive woman on his arm. Other women passersby looked at him in surprise, then stared with envy at the vision of feminine fashion accompanying him. He had no idea where she wanted to go and didn't care as long as she let him go with her.

"Surely, your parents did not christen you Goose?" she prompted.

"No, ma'am, but it's been so long since anyone's called me by anything else that I wouldn't know how to respond if someone did actually call my name."

She tilted her head back to look at him from beneath the brim of her hat, tipped low and angled rakishly over one eye. Goose doubted any other lady in Copperhead Gulch had such dashing style. "Well, you look nothing like a bad-tempered waterfowl, so I'd much rather have your real name."

Goose's breath caught in his massive chest as he considered this verbal intimacy. Emboldened, he replied, "Only if you allow me to call you Angelica."

She blinked in surprise and recovered. "That's only fair. Please, do call me Angelica. I only share such intimacies with my greatest friends and now I shall count you among that select group."

"Angus MacDonald," he replied, dismayed that she regarded him as a friend rather than as a suitor. His conscience rebuked him: *Suitor? What do you have to offer such a fine lady?*

"Oh, your family comes from Scotland then?"

"My pa," he replied as they walked toward the boarding house at the outer edge of the small town. With misgivings, he decided to come clean. "My ma's native."

"Native? You mean an Indian?"

He nodded. "She's good people though."

Those gloved fingers patted his arm again, a small, discreet gesture of reassurance. "I don't doubt it if she produced such a good man as you. My own father is French and my mother was a free mulatto—" she patted a glossy dark curl "—so I've no cause to disparage anyone's ancestry."

He frowned at the admission of a pedigree that would alienate less open-minded folks and said, "I wouldn't go telling folks hereabouts about that."

Her full lips curled at the corners in a small, sad smile. "I won't. I don't normally tell anyone about my personal life. It's not safe for a woman living alone and supporting herself."

In fact, she thought, Cousin Horace was one of the reasons it wasn't safe for people to know of her mother, especially east of the Mississippi River. Just because the War Between the States had abolished slavery did not mean that anyone with African blood could expect respect, equal treatment, or even common courtesy. Cousin Horace, the legitimate son of her white grandfather's youngest daughter, was a pain in her exquisitely attired posterior.

They walked in companionable silence for a little while longer.

"Angelica, what did you plan on doing the rest of the day?" Goose asked when they reached the boarding house.

"I intended to sit on the back porch of this establishment and spend a few hours reading." She grinned at him. "And, to be perfectly wicked, I'm going to remove my shoes."

She extended one elegantly clad foot from beneath the hem of her dress. Goose's eyes widened as his thoughts immediately shot to removing other garments from the lovely shape they covered. He swallowed, the sound audible.

"They pinch," she confessed in a husky whisper, then giggled like a little girl.

Goose gulped again, imagining other things that pinched, like her corset. He barely managed to stifle a groan at the mental image of her plump bosom unfettered by her corset, freed of their cloth prison.

They stopped at the boarding house's front door. Angelica removed her hand from his arm and thanked him for his safe escort.

"Um ... will you be joining us at poker tonight?" he blurted.

She gave him another sad little smile of regret. "I believe I wore out my welcome with Mr. Cordoba, so I'll have to see if another table will accept me."

Afraid of the prospect that he wouldn't have the opportunity to enjoy her company again, Goose invited her to join his game anyway. "I won't let 'em deny you a seat, Angelica. They're just jealous of your skills."

She patted his arm again. "Angus, I'm a card sharp trained from childhood by my father, the notorious Philippe Durand. There might be three or four people on this continent who can beat me at any card game. Since we are now the greatest of friends, I do not want to take your money."

Goose thought of the money he'd recently deposited at the bank in Copperhead Gulch and at other banks in other towns where he stopped by to deliver hides and game and those special herbs that whites like to use in their medicines but couldn't recognize growing from the ground. He had his mother to thank for that. He thought of the burbling stream where he sometimes panned for gold, the soft, yellow metal for which his mother's people had no use and his father hadn't lived long enough to discover.

For the first time ever, Goose wondered if he could tolerate the transition from living amid nature's glory to living in a dirty, dusty, smelly town. His heart sank, because he knew the crowd of people and the filthy conditions would crush his soul. He also knew that this lovely, sophisticated woman had no place among his mother's people, nor would she withstand his own hard way of life.

"Angus? Angus?"

He blinked, recalled from his musing by her soft voice.

"Where did you go, Angus?" she asked.

Flushing with embarrassment, he coughed, shook his head, and excused himself. "I'll come fetch you for our card game about seven o'clock this evening."

She bowed to the inevitable. "Very well, Angus. I'll be waiting for you."

She watched as he clomped down the steps of the front porch and walked away to tend to his own business. The poor man had made such an effort to impress her. She was touched, charmed even. It had been a long time since anyone made such an effort for her, certainly not since ... no, she would not think of that. *Put it from your mind.*

She headed inside and did as she said she would do after taking off her hat and changing into a loose dress infinitely more comfortable than the stylish dress in which she'd paraded around town. She had no doubt she'd receive at least half a dozen inquiries from ladies asking about her fashionable garb. With a small smile, she made sure several of her sister's business cards were tucked in her handbag. Marie would appreciate the referrals and additional business.

With Mama's hands twisted and bent from arthritis, she depended entirely upon Marie and what income Angelica could send them. Papa had too little concern for his mistress and their younger daughter who cared naught for card games or any other sort of gambling.

Angelica looked down at her new book and knew she shouldn't have wasted the money on it, but sometimes— just like Papa—she couldn't resist temptation. *No matter. I'll just have to win that money and more back tonight.*

Her belly growled long before she expected Goose to escort her to the saloon for another night of gambling. She begged a couple of biscuits left over from breakfast and a glass of milk from the boarding house's proprietress, paying an additional two pennies for the meal. With a conspiratorial wink, the African cook and maid-of-all-work—who also hailed from New Orleans—slipped her an early plum, too. They shared a short, friendly conversation that mainly revolved around her father's particular favorite dish, *lapin à la moutarde.*

She ate in her room, careful not to leave any crumbs behind, as she put that morning's dress back on. Looking at her travel trunk, she acknowledged that a trip to the town's laundry was necessary. She hoped that the laundress knew how to treat such fine fabrics as she wore.

When Goose knocked on the door, she stood ready and waiting for him in the front parlor. The proprietress who sat in a chair with her mending threw her a disapproving glare and muttered something under her breath about brazen hussies. Angelica ignored her and greeted Goose with a smile and friendly words. She stepped into the shade of the front porch, closing the door behind her.

"Are you ready?" he asked and doffed his new hat. He felt like a fool, but wanted to show her he could look and act like a fancy gentleman.

She placed her hand on his arm and, tilting her head up to look at him as they walked, said, "Angus, we are friends, are we not?"

"Of course. Why?"

"Because I do not want you to take offense."

"Why would I take offense?"

She chuckled and his groin tightened at the low, husky sound. "I cannot help but think that you purchased that hat to impress me."

In the lingering sunlight of late summer, she could see the tops of his ears turn red. She patted his arm.

"You don't need to do that. I can recognize a good, honest, and kind man. You don't need to don fancy clothes to impress me."

"I don't?" he blurted.

"Of course not," she reassured him. "If I wanted a fancy man, I would have accepted Mr. Cordoba's escort last night."

At the mention of the other man's name, Goose frowned. He hadn't liked the way Jesse spoke to her, hadn't liked the way Jesse looked at her. "He suspects who you are."

"Of course, he does. And I recognized his name as well. He's a skilled opponent. It's a small circle in which I travel, really. Professional gamblers who are successful at making a decent living aren't all that common."

"I thought you hadn't met him before."

"I was thirteen years old, a little girl traveling with her father. He didn't notice me."

Goose gaped at the thought of the gambler exposing his innocent daughter to the ugliness of saloon after saloon.

"I learned at an early age to read people," she admitted. "Papa often relied on my observations."

"And your observations of Jesse Cordoba?" he prompted.

"Skilled, calculating, and unforgiving."

Goose nodded. "He plays fair, though."

"True. He doesn't cheat at cards."

Goose wondered if she were damning the other man with faint praise. "What about Chester MacAllister?"

She tapped her chin. "He's a professional gambler, but not as successful as he thinks he should be. He resents losing, but doesn't have the skill to cheat without getting caught. If he were interested in my opinion, I'd suggest he find himself other employment."

Goose choked down a laugh.

"Will it be just the four of us tonight at the table, or do you know if someone else is joining us?"

He shrugged. "I dunno. Ain't many folks who'll gamble at the stakes we play."

"Ah," she said. "So, the stakes increase tonight."

"I didn't say that."

"But they will," she predicted with a wise expression.

Indeed they did. Sitting next to Angelica, he watched her carefully as she charmed the men at the table, offered tantalizing glimpses of creamy skin, ran her fingers up and down the buttons of her bodice, touched the glossy shine of her curls, and chewed on her full bottom lip. By the end of the first hour of play, no man sitting at the table and several of those sitting at other tables could tear his eyes off her. Many sported obvious erections. Goose was no exception.

The men's enthrallment initially annoyed the whores who plied their trade in the saloon, but soon the whores enjoyed a brisk business as those men, denied their original goal, settled for the available alternative.

Goose watched as Angelica played with sublime skill, showing pleasing graciousness whether losing or winning a hand. The hours passed and the pile of money in front of her increased until Chester threw down his cards and called it quits.

"Lady Luck is not my friend tonight," he said and headed for the bar to drown his sorrows in cheap rotgut.

Angelica and Jesse exchanged glances, eyes narrowed.

"Shall we continue, or have you finished playing as well?" she challenged him.

He waved a hand in a languid gesture that attempted to hide his growing ire. "Ladies first."

She chuckled, the sultry sound stirring the blood of every man in hearing distance. "Oh, no, I'm having too much fun to quit now."

"Deal," the gambler ordered Albert.

With a sigh, Albert shuffled and dealt, using the same deck of cards that Angelica brought the night before. A small line appeared between her arched eyebrows as she rubbed her ungloved fingertip along the edge of one card.

"Mr. Derringer, has anyone handled these cards between yesterday's game and today's?"

Albert shrugged.

"You will agree that the cards yesterday were brand new and had not been tampered with when I handed them to you?"

Both Albert and Goose nodded. After a moment, Jesse nodded, too.

She ran a sensitive fingertip along the edge of the card. Then she tested the edges and surface of the other cards in her hand. Looking up at Albert, she lay her cards face down on the table and said, "These cards have been marked."

Jesse leaned back and regarded her with suspicion. "Don't you think it's odd that you're the only one to discover cheating here two nights in a row—cheating that, I might add, no one else even suspected? And wouldn't you have had ample opportunity to mark the cards as you held them?"

Angelica's spine and shoulders stiffened with affront.

"I do not *need* to cheat, Mr. Cordoba. That's why I bring a pack of new cards to each new table of players and leave it with the dealer. That ensures fair play, especially necessary when it's difficult enough to persuade a group of men to allow *me* to join their table. They assume I could not win honestly."

Goose fingered his cards, but his callused fingertips could not discern any subtle alterations. He looked at Jesse and shrugged.

"I can't tell," he admitted. With a grunt, he added, "I believe her."

Jesse sighed and fingered the cards in his own hand. He frowned, then glowered with simmering rage as his own sensitive fingers detected the barely-there differences. He looked at the dealer and snapped, "Albert?"

Turning pale, the dealer said, "I didn't mark no cards, honest. The boss keeps all decks of cards in his office. Someone else must've done it."

"Marking cards this subtly takes skill," Jesse remarked and glared at Angelica. "Skill which we both know you possess."

"I did *not* mark the cards," Angelica protested.

"Well, I defy any woman to beat me without using tricks," Jesse stated. "Even the daughter of Philippe Durand."

Albert coughed. "You're Durand's daughter?"

Affecting a haughty pride that any duchess could claim, she replied, "Yes, I am Philippe Durand's daughter, which is why I do *not* need the assistance of marked cards."

"You're a woman; deceit is natural," Jesse scoffed.

Angelica stood and glared at the man. "I will not stay where I'm not wanted. If you'll excuse me, gentlemen?"

Jesse's hand snapped out and landed on her forearm as she collected her winnings. His grip tightened over her sleeve and, therefore, the small, slender knife concealed beneath the fabric. "You'll leave your money at the table."

An ominous *click* from Chester's direction announced that he'd drawn a small pistol in solidarity with Jesse. Goose watched the tableau unfold and wondered what he could do that wouldn't get either of them shot for stupidity.

She fixed both men with a hard look. "I won that money, fair and square. I'll not leave it behind."

"You will."

"Unhand me, you brute," she hissed.

"Take your filthy hands off the money and leave it. You forfeit your winnings, bitch."

"Let her go, Jesse," Goose rumbled. "She ain't no liar and she ain't no cheater."

Jesse chuckled, an ugly sound of derision. "She's got you snookered, you idiot. What'd she do? Let you touch her pretty tits and promise you more if you went along with her scheme?"

Angelica gasped in outrage and tried to yank her arm from Jesse's grasp.

"Angelica didn't promise me nothin'," Goose replied as he lumbered to his feet. "Let her go, Jesse, and let her have her stake back. I'll see she gets back to the boarding house safely."

"That's not fair," she hissed, appalled at being forced to leave twenty times her stake at the table. She looked up at Goose. "I did *not* cheat."

He just shook his head. "You were right, Angelica. I shouldn't have persuaded you to play a second night."

Jesse laughed. "Oh, you besotted fool!" He released her arm. "Take the bitch and go, Goose. She ain't welcome here no more." His eyes narrowed. "And she forfeits *everything*, including her stake."

Goose tugged her to her feet and drew her out of the saloon. "I'm sorry, Angelica. Let me make it up to you."

Her shoulders sagged in defeat. "You left your money at the table, too, Goose. Besides, I cannot ask you to cover my loss."

"Albert'll hold my money for me," he said, not believing in that for a second.

"Goose, you're in no position to pay me what I won, and I wouldn't accept the money from you anyway."

"I can afford it."

She gave him a sad little smile and shook her head in disbelief. She patted his arm and said, "The offer is kind and generous, but I cannot accept. I'll be leaving tomorrow."

She lapsed into silence and resolved to find a laundry in the next town where she landed.

"Where will you go?" he asked after a long moment.

"North, I suppose. Wherever the wind blows me."

Heart sinking, Goose offered to escort her to the stagecoach stop the next morning. She patted his arm again and accepted the offer with gentle gratitude.

At dawn the following day, Angus appeared on the front porch of the boarding house as promised and carried the larger of her two bags as he escorted her to the depot where the stagecoach waited. The four horses restive horses danced in the traces, eager to unleash their energy. Goose handed her traveling case and hatbox to the driver's assistant who tied to the back of the big coach.

Goose and Angelica stopped and faced each other. He tried to smile, but couldn't. She kissed her gloved fingertips, then raised them to his cheek as the driver shouted for all passengers to climb aboard.

"I'll say *au revoir*, not goodbye," she told him as she boarded the stagecoach, "because I always hope to see my dearest friends again."

Two days later, Angelica pressed her scented handkerchief to her nose in a futile effort to block out the stench of the two passengers sitting at either side of her as the stagecoach lurched and rattled along a bumpy road. She bent her head over the book purchased the day before and hoped it would entertain her sufficiently during the long drive. The only other female passenger in the vehicle cast curious glances at her, taking in every detail of Angelica's traveling costume. Marie had outdone herself with that particular outfit.

The woman, however, did not seem to appreciate Marie's fine work, but seemed resentful. *Perhaps she's just envious.* The woman tugged on her husband's sleeve and whispered none too softly in a broad southern drawl, "Since the War of Northern Aggression, these stagecoach companies will accept *anyone's* custom. Disgraceful, if you ask me."

Angelica closed her eyes, then opened them again as a meaty hand landed on her thigh.

"Sir, you are too familiar," she said in an icy tone. She closed the book with a snap.

He leered at her, then said, "Woman like you travelin' alone, I know what you do to earn them fancy clothes. How much?"

He didn't remove his hand, but instead squeezed the flesh beneath the layers of cloth.

Exhaling forcefully through her nose, she glanced at the other passengers. *Nope, no help forthcoming from them.* Unfortunately, that odious man was not the first— nor would he be the last—to assume liberties to which he had no right.

"Sir, you are incorrect. Even if I were such a woman, I'd decline you as a customer, because I'd never be that desperate." She smacked his hand with the book, the sound loud even in the creaking, rattling vehicle. "*Now remove your hand from my person.*"

The man's ruddy face flushed even darker with embarrassment as the two other male passengers on the stagecoach guffawed at the insult. However, crammed like sardines in the vehicle, he could not very well rape her. Muttering dire threats pertaining to her alleged—and undoubtedly nonexistent—virtue, he tore his hand away, but not without swiping it against her breast.

"Touch me again and I'll gut you," Angelica threatened.

"Uppity whore," the man muttered.

"If you dressed appropriate to your station, girl, then men such as that would not take liberties," the woman declared with a haughty sniff.

"My station?" Angelica echoed.

The woman tugged on her husband's sleeve again. "Really, Mr. Ambrust, I cannot abide riding in such proximity to one such as that woman. You must speak to the coachman directly to rectify this untenable situation."

The woman's husband looked at Angelica and licked his lips, eyes gleaming with greed. She knew that look and often exploited the urges behind it—but only at the card table. She also knew that the man would do nothing while his wife was present.

What she did not know was that he would speak to the driver when the stagecoach stopped at the next station and that he and the passenger whom she insulted would convince the driver to evict her from the vehicle. Fuming with offense, Angelica soon found herself standing on the dusty excuse for a highway with hatbox in one hand and traveling trunk at her feet as she glared at the stagecoach rolling away from her in a cloud of dust. She looked back at the grizzled old man who staffed the way station and took care of the horses.

"Ain't got no place fer the likes o' you to stay, missy. You'd best be gettin' on." He spat a stream of tobacco juice that landed just inches from the hem of her skirt.

"And just what do you expect me to do?" she wondered aloud.

"Don't much care," the man said. He shrugged and lowered the bucket into the well. "I got no taste fer yer kind."

Angelica looked at the travel case and contemplated its contents. With the twenty-five pound weight limit specified by the stagecoach company, the trunk did not contain much. Still, its bulk made it cumbersome and not easily carried by hand. She considered her limited options, none of them good.

"May I store my trunk here until it can be retrieved?"

The man's eyes gleamed with greed. "It'll cost ya a penny per day."

Angelica eyes narrowed with anger. "That's usury. I'll pay a nickel per week, four weeks in advance."

The old man grunted and looked the finely dressed woman up and down. He figured she had at least one more fancy dress like that in the trunk, which he could sell for a lot more than a measly twenty cents. He grunted again and said, "Rate just went up to two bits per week."

Angelica fumed. With a curt nod to feign acceptance, she dragged the trunk toward the shack where the old man lived. She announced, "I'll change into something more practical, then leave the trunk in your safekeeping."

The man nodded and returned to fetching water for the livestock. His employer's success depended upon healthy livestock.

Dragging the trunk into the ramshackle building, Angelica wrinkled her nose at the filthy, stinking conditions inside the shack and cringed at the cockroaches boldly creeping across the floor. She opened her trunk and pulled out the loose, comfortable dress she'd worn two days before while reading on the boarding house's back porch. She quickly changed from the fine traveling costume to that much more practical dress. Unfortunately, she could do little about her footwear: she had a choice of a fine pair of half-boots and a fine pair of shoes. She kept the boots. She left her jewelry in the trunk: the glass and jet beads were pretty, but inexpensive. Papa taught her long ago never to carry valuable jewelry. She tucked her money about her person, the loose dress containing a variety of small pockets sewn unobtrusively into the garment. Marie was a genius at such things. Pursing her lips, she dropped her pepper-box revolver down an easy-to-reach pocket and checked to make sure the knife concealed under her sleeve remained ready to use. She pulled out her shawl and looped the ribbons of her reticule around her wrist.

She opened her hatbox and swapped out the stylish hat inside it for some more practical items: stockings, a chemise, handkerchiefs, ammunition for the small pistol, and her book. For some reason, she could not bear to leave the book behind. It reminded her of Goose's kindness.

Finally, Angelica closed the trunk and locked it. The lock wouldn't stop that nasty old man from busting the trunk itself to get to the contents, but that was the best she could do.

She dropped twenty-five cents on the crudely fashioned table and left, figuring that if she didn't return within a week to retrieve her belongings, then the old coot could have them. She cringed as a cockroach scuttled over the toe of her boot.

Adjusting her grasp on the handle of the hatbox, Angelica called out, "Your fee's on the table."

The old man finished pouring a bucketful of water into the trough and nodded.

"No place to go but forward," she murmured to herself. Resolved to make the best of a bad situation, she walked in the direction taken by the stagecoach. Surely, she'd encounter a village along the way. Perhaps, she'd even come across people who subscribed to the concept of simple human decency.

Blisters formed on her heel before she'd walked three miles and on the balls of her feet before she'd finished five miles. She knew that blood, as red as any white man's, soaked through her stockings. The hatbox pulled at her arms and shoulders, its weight seeming to increase with every step. As her skirt wrapped around her legs, she wished—not for the first time—that she'd been born male.

"Wish in one hand and shit in the other, then see which hand fills up faster," she muttered under her breath, quoting her mama's bitter, homespun wisdom.

She spent a cold and hungry night beside the so-called road, hardly sleeping a wink due to fear of being accosted by wildlife of either the two- or four-legged variety. She saw nothing threatening, except the clouds overhead as they gathered and darkened.

The temperature dropped and rain began to fall. Shivering, chilled, and drenched, Angelica slogged along the muddy road and hoped that a passerby would exercise some charity and offer her a ride to the next village. Her wishes went unanswered: apparently, nothing but the stagecoach traveled that road. She spent another miserable night alone and hungry.

The next morning, she persevered through sheer force of will. Surely, she would find human habitation this day. Clutching the hatbox as though her life depended upon it, the exhausted woman staggered forth.

Not for the first time did Goose chastise himself for a fool as his thoughts once again dwelled upon the lovely face and form of a certain female card sharp. He tugged on the strap anchoring the load of furs on his mule's back, making sure the weight was evenly distributed and secure. He rolled his shoulders beneath the broad straps of the packs he carried. Satisfied that he'd made himself and Beulah as comfortable as possible, he resumed leading the beast toward the poor excuse of a road that would take him the most direct route into Shipshead. He snorted, using the small town's unlikely name to distract his thoughts. *Ain't nobody there's ever been on a ship and there ain't no lake nearby big enough for a ship, so why'd they name the place like that?*

The speculation entertained him for the next few minutes as he trudged along the narrow deer path leading from the mountains to the broad plain where he'd take the road. Wet from the day's rain, the footing underneath his feet and Beulah's hooves proved treacherous and slowed their progress. That, of course, gave Beulah additional time to examine their surroundings and take offense at imagined threats through which Goose had to coax her with sweet words and promises of sugar cubes.

Finally, the mule planted her feet and refused to budge. Her head went upward, her big ears pointed forward, and her velvety nostrils flared. The whites of her eyes showed.

"What is it, Beulah?" he asked, making sure to keep his voice low and soft. Insulting the beast would get them nowhere. The mule exhaled forcefully through her nostrils. He tugged on the rope connected to her halter. "Ain't nothing there, Beulah. Let's go."

The mule did not budge. Goose knew that no amount of pulling would move that mule: she could be persuaded, not forced. The jennet quivered, a strange whining sound coming from her that Goose recognized as being indicative of something truly worth his attention.

"What is it, girl?" he asked as he peered around them, searching for the danger or anomaly that Beulah detected with her keen senses. He listened, wary and still, and heard nothing more than the drip-drop of water falling from leaves, the soughing of the cold breeze, and the muffled cry and grunt of a—*What the hell?*

"Stay put," he ordered the mule and dropped the lead rope and the packs he shouldered. Rushing forward, Goose scrambled down the hillside, grabbing onto saplings and bushes on the way down to steady his headlong progress. His enormous chest heaved when he reached the bottom and peered at the dirty, sodden heap of fabric collapsed near the edge of a gully etched into the earth where the foot of the hill met the plain. He watched a case teeter on the crumbling edge and fall into dirty water from the past day's rain rushing through the narrow channel. It was deep enough to drown the weak or unwary. He wasn't going after it, and hoped the woman had nothing terribly valuable in it.

With a grunt, he leaped across the gully and went to whoever had collapsed on its soft, crumbling edge. He did not look to see whom he rescued, but merely grabbed a convenient limb and hauled the woman away from the treacherous edge. When he considered them safe from the collapse of waterlogged dirt, he rolled the woman over and gasped in horror. Her tangled hair had long since escaped its pins. Her plain dress was damp and muddy, torn at the hem. Dark smudges beneath her eyes looked like bruises.

"Angelica?" He shook her gently. She moaned, but did not open her eyes. "Angelica!"

Her eyes fluttered open, but he saw only delirium, not recognition.

"I am dead," she whispered.

"Not if I can help it," he growled. Lumbering to his feet, he hoisted the woman over his shoulder and clamped her in place with one arm wrapped around her thighs. He eyed the gully and the road running beside it to where the gully bent just before widening into a real river. He wondered if he ought to walk the half mile to the bridge or try to jump the span.

"Ah, hell," he muttered and decided to trudge the half mile to the bridge, practical, not dashing. *Well, a man shouldn't risk his life just to appear brave for a woman who's unconscious anyway.* He looked skyward. *At least it stopped raining.*

The walk back up the hill took four times as long as the headlong slide down; however, Beulah remained right where he'd told her to wait. Goose dug in a leather pouch to retrieve a couple of sugar cubes to reward the jennet for her patient obedience before making room among the load of furs to lay the woman. He used a length of extra rope to tie her in place so she wouldn't roll off and tumble downhill.

She did not regain consciousness during the careful trek that angled down the side of the big hill. The slope flattened when it reached a rudimentary bridge connecting a seldom used road between Shipshead and the village of Farol Verde to the west. The sound of rushing water below did not drown the hollow sound of Beulah's hoofbeats on the heavy planks of wood.

After they crossed the bridge, Goose found a sheltered, relatively dry place to rest. Tending to Angelica would cost him at least half a day's travel, but he could not at all resent doing so. Beulah looked content to cut her day's work short.

In short order, he fashioned a soft pallet forAngelica, sacrificing three deerskins and two wolfskins to her comfort. He felt a momentary pang of regret for the loss of income, then reminded himself that he had enough money to satisfy his simple needs. Truly. He glanced at the lovely woman who lay motionless on the bed of furs and wondered how much money it took to satisfy a woman like that.

Goose's belly rumbled, reminding him that he hadn't eaten since breakfast. He scrounged around to find wood dry enough to burn without choking them in smoke. When he had a small campfire going, he pulled out dried meat, dried beans, bacon, and coffee from his packs and soon had a small pot of stew simmering and a pot of coffee boiling.

Perhaps it was the fragrance of food that brought Angelica back to consciousness. She groaned, which brought Goose to her side. He smoothed her hair away from her face and murmured soothing nonsense words at her.

"What? Where am I?" Her eyes fluttered open, vision blurry. When she focused on the man holding her, she gasped. "Angus?"

"What happened, Angelica?"

Her pretty lips assumed a bitter twist. "Nothing I shouldn't have anticipated." She inhaled. "Is that coffee I smell?"

He nodded. "Stew, too, if you think you could eat something."

Her belly growled. "I could eat an entire cow right now."

He felt abashed with the strange sensation that he'd already failed her. "It's venison."

She smiled at him, the blatant gratitude making his heart pound. "Oh, venison would be lovely, too."

"I ... um ... I have some ... um ... would you like some?"

Her smile broadened. "Yes, thank you, Angus. I would love some."

He filled his tin plate and handed it and his spoon to her. She ate with delicate manners as befitted a lady, but left him in no doubt of her hunger as she scraped the plate clean. He filled his tin mug with coffee and handed that to her. She sipped it with a happy sigh of gratitude and pleasure. She handed the plate, spoon, and cup back to him when she finished.

"How long has it been since you ate?" he asked after refilling it and digging into his own supper.

"At least two days," she answered. "I really am grateful for your assistance."

"Did something happen to the stagecoach?" he asked as he filled his plate and ate. He thought there was something wonderfully intimate about putting the spoon she'd used into his own mouth. He fancied he could taste her on the metal.

Her shoulders sagged. "They kicked me off."

"But why?"

Angelica cast him a wry glance that hinted he ought to know why. "A woman traveling alone encounters certain ... *assumptions* ... offensive to respectable folks. Others resent when those assumptions prove false."

He muttered a word under his breath that no gentleman spoke in a lady's presence. Angling his face away from her, he cleaned the empty plate and stowed them among his packs. He needed the time to master his emotions and affect a composed and confident presence. Finally, he asked, "What do you intend to do?"

Belly filled and warm, she pondered that. "I had intended to walk to the next town and purchase another stagecoach ticket."

"Going where?"

Her shoulders sagged. "I'm not entirely sure. It seems to get more difficult every time to sit in on a card game. I've no other way to make my living unless I want to become a whore—and I *don't*."

"What about your pa?"

"Papa died about six months ago, not enough time for word to have spread to a lot of the smaller towns. Sometimes, I can get into a game on the strength of being Philippe Durand's daughter. Folks want to boast that they beat me in a card game because they can then say they bested 'Durand' without specifying the father or the daughter."

Goose frowned at her cynicism. It didn't seem right that a young, pretty woman such as she should affect such a world-weary attitude. Still, perhaps he could use her unfortunate circumstances to his advantage.

"I'm headed to Shipshead. Got business there," he said. "I'd be honored if you'd keep me company."

Angelica tilted her head to the side as she considered the polite invitation. "Do you really want me along or are you just being polite?"

"We're friends, right?"

"Of course, Angus."

"Then I want your company."

She smiled, an open and joyous expression devoid of the usual calculation. His mouth went dry. *God, she's gorgeous!* Other parts of him took notice, too. He shifted uncomfortably.

Angelica noticed him noticing her and took pity rather than exploiting his attraction as her father had taught her. "Do you think I might have a large bowl of water, perhaps some soap and a cloth?"

"What for?"

She sighed again, because men never seemed to understand—at least not the men of her acquaintance. "I'm filthy. I'd like to wash and see if I can't clean some of my clothes, too."

A blush pricked his skin beneath the heavy scruff of his beard. "I should have remembered that ladies like to be clean."

She gave him a soft smile. "Yes, we do. Tiresome creatures, aren't we?"

"Not really." The heated blush turned fiery as he blurted. "I like the way you smell."

Angelica's own cheeks deepened in color. "Er … thank you."

Goose rubbed his broad palms over his face. "I ain't got no soap with me, but I can give you some clean water and a cloth to use."

He untied the bandana around his neck and handed it to her.

Her grateful smile made him feel ten feet tall. He bustled about to fulfill his promise as she moved behind a cluster of shrubs for privacy, every mincing step a silent testament to discomfort. Determined not to take undue advantage, he still could not help peeking at her when he handed her a bucket of water and that promised rag. That sweet, tantalizing glimpse of soft, creamy, womanly flesh nearly caused him to swallow his tongue. Her sigh of pleasure as she washed off the gritty residue of her trek made him wish his trousers were larger.

"Angus!"

"What is it?" he called back, mortified that his words came out a few octaves higher than normal.

"Do you have a length of cloth or an extra shirt I might borrow for tonight? I want to wash my clothes as best I can and set them out to dry."

He visibly shivered as temptation gripped him in its claws. He considered what he had available and drew out a clean shirt, the new shirt he'd purchased to impress her just a few days ago. Squinting his eyes and averting his gaze, he sidled toward the bushes and dangled the shirt from his fingertips.

"Will this do?"

"Oh, how lovely! I'll be sure to repay your generosity somehow."

He knew how he wanted her to repay his generosity, but honor forbade demanding that.

Angelica hissed as she drew off her stockings and examined the bloody mess.

"Are you all right, Angelica?" Goose called out when he heard the noise of distress.

"Blisters," she replied.

"Where?"

"My feet."

He winced. "You put that shirt on and let me treat those blisters, else they'll fester. You don't want that, Angel."

Angelica's eyes widened at the shortening of her name. She'd always discouraged such familiarity, but found she liked it on this kind man's tongue. She finished stripping and cleaning her body, then slipped on the shirt. The long sleeves dangled past her hands and the hem would likely hang past her knees. It would have to do to preserve her modesty.

"I'm ready," she called and tried to rise. Pain shot through her bare feet and she whimpered.

"You stay put," he ordered as he rushed toward her. He glanced at the sodden wad of bloodstained fabric he correctly assumed were her stockings and stifled a wince. He scooped her into his arms and said, "I'll carry you."

"Thank you, Angus," she said as she wrapped her arms around his neck, knowing that pride had no place here.

He carried her back to the pallet of animal hides and set her down, giving her a moment to arrange the shirt for modesty. Squatting at her feet, he took one in his hands. That time he did wince.

"This is bad, Angel."

She sighed. "My boots weren't made for extended hikes across the country."

"It's best if you stay barefoot and off those feet to let 'em heal."

"I can hardly walk to Shipshead without shoes."

"You can ride Beulah."

"Beulah?"

He gestured with his chin. "My mule."

"Doesn't she have more than enough to carry?"

Angus frowned at the stubborn nature of this woman. "She carried you from the gully all the way to here."

"Point taken," Angelica conceded. "How far is it to Shipshead?"

"About another full day's travel." He set her foot down and turned to rummage in his packs. After a moment, he withdrew a small gourd, dipped his finger inside, and came up with an off-putting lump of grease. He picked up her foot again and said, "My ma taught me how to make this ointment. It'll help heal those blisters and prevent infection."

She nodded as he smeared the grease over her blistered skin. The initial touch of the grease stung and made her wince, then a soothing coolness sank into the damaged flesh.

Angus heard her sigh, looked up from her foot, and grinned. "Feels good, don't it?"

"Indeed. Smells atrocious, though."

He shrugged, put her foot down and picked up the other to treat. When he finished, he looked at her face again and noticed how worn and tired she appeared.

"You rest. We'll sit put here until tomorrow."

She yawned, covering her mouth with a slender, elegant hand. "I don't want to delay your schedule any more than I already have."

He shook his head. "I ain't on no schedule."

She sighed and returned a sleepy smile. "Then I'd be delighted to stay here until tomorrow morning."

He nodded, liking the pleasure and satisfaction that taking care of her gave him. "You get some rest and I'll keep watch."

"Watch?"

"We're in Indian territory, Angel. Lucky for us, my ma's tribe roams here and ain't likely to bother us none." His expression darkened. "They're generally peaceable, 'cept settlers like to rile 'em up and then blame them for violence."

He looked to see her reaction, but she'd already fallen asleep. He extracted his blanket from his packs and drew it over her. While she slept, he tidied the campsite and took care of Beulah who'd endured being ignored with exemplary patience.

"I never saw a woman so pretty," he whispered to the mule. Beulah's big ears swiveled. Doubt assailed him and he echoed Jesse Cordoba's words, "You think ... nah. Nah, fancy woman like that don't want the likes of me."

Sticking close to the woman he'd rapidly come to consider as *his*, Angus found himself bored with nothing to do but imagine crawling onto that pallet next to her and running his callused palms over that sweet flesh. He licked his lips and wondered how it would feel to kiss her, to *taste* her. She shifted in her sleep, dislodging the blanket. The shirt crept up, revealing plump thighs. He swallowed a groan.

Beulah stamped a hoof and snorted, distracting his attention. He sent the mule a grateful look and peered into the distance to see what had disturbed the usually placid beast. He smiled at the sight of a pheasant surveying its surroundings. Angus eased his rifle from the scabbard attached to Beulah's harness and leveled it into position. Weapon always loaded, he aimed and fired.

Angelica woke with a scream at the crack of noise. Blinking in fear, she gathered her wits as quickly as she could and huffed when she saw the big man going after whatever it was he'd shot. She lay back down to resume her nap. *Stupid man didn't even think that I'd wake at a gunshot. I hope it was worth it.*

It was.

The smell of pheasant roasting over a fire woke her again.

"Here, you eat first," he said, offering her a loaded plate. It felt good to provide for his woman.

With murmured thanks, she accepted the food and ate. He took the plate from her, refilled it, and finished off the carcass. Watching him eat, she realized that a big man like that needed a lot of fuel.

"My mama would enjoy feeding a man like you," she commented.

He wiped his mouth with the back of his sleeve and grinned at her. "My ma claims I eat more than any three braves."

Her gaze wandered over him, taking in the heavy bulge of muscle, flat stomach, tree trunk thighs. She felt heat pool low in her belly and her pulse quicken. With his thick, still short beard, he reminded her of the fabled giant Paul Bunyan, a handsome, virile version who didn't need a blue ox to impress the men and woo the ladies.

"Where do you live?" she asked.

He swallowed a gulp of scalding coffee and put down the tin mug to answer. "I got a place in the mountains. It ain't much, small." His eyes brightened. "I been meaning to add a room or two, make it bigger."

Angelica nodded and looked around. "It's peaceful up there, I suppose?"

He nodded. "Sure is. Wolves sing at night through the winter. It's a right pretty sound, if mournful. In the spring, peepers sing."

"Peepers?"

"Frogs. My cabin sits near a pond. Good fishing in that pond."

She nodded. He felt obligated to make the place sound as good as he could.

"In the fall, the trees turn gold, real pretty. Right now it's all green. Deer walk through with their fawns, all delicate and pretty like you. Sometimes I'll see a grizzly bear. That's an awesome sight. They're huge and powerful. I got me a bearskin rug. It's nice underfoot in the winter."

"It sounds lovely."

He noticed the wistful tone to her words.

"I—I could take you up with me. Maybe you'd like it. I'd like to think you would."

She smiled, but the expression struck him as melancholy rather than joyous. "You don't want to do that."

"Why not?"

"First, I've no notion how to conduct myself in such wilderness. Second, it wouldn't be appropriate."

Resolve sparked and hardened. "Then marry me, Angel."

Her smile dimmed. "What?"

He swallowed. Hard. "Marry me. I ain't never met a woman I fancy as much as you." He swallowed again, aware his words lacked persuasion. "I'd be a good husband, faithful to you. And I'll build rooms onto the cabin, make it bigger. Really, I will."

She shook her head. "Angus, you don't want a quadroon for a wife, especially a card sharp."

He scooted closer to her and took her hand in his, liking the way it nestled against his big paw. "Angel, I'm a half-breed. Even if I fancied any other woman, no respectable woman would have me. My ma's folks don't much care, but I trade mostly with the whites. I'd ... I'd protect you, keep you safe, give you children."

She blinked, stunned at his generosity. "I have nothing to give you, nothing to reciprocate."

However, he did not hear her softly spoken objection. Words continued to roll from his tongue. "I ain't 'xactly poor. Folks don't realize that, but I can afford them fripperies women like so much."

She set her other hand on his forearm, the heat seeming to burn through the fabric and brand him. "And where would I wear those fripperies?" She sighed. "I can't see you moving into town, any town, Angus."

He met her gaze, his direct, honest, and unflinching. It shamed her. "All I'd ask is that you be faithful to me, Angel, that you be my woman and no one else's. If you need to live in town, then I'd support you."

She hung her head, then met his gaze with candor and regret. "I couldn't ask you to make such a sacrifice, Angus. I'm not worth it."

He pressed his lips together in a thin line of disagreement, but said nothing more other than to bid her get some rest.

Angelica nodded and lay back down and listened to the sounds of her suitor tidying up the campsite again. It felt *good* to have someone take care of her. Even as a child, she'd tended to her father's needs: the man wouldn't have picked up his own socks if God himself had ordered it. Papa had liked having his girl fetch and carry for him, see to his laundry and meals, and make his life comfortable.

Their conversation did not resume the next morning. All business, Angus cut off the stained bodice from the skirt of her only dress and turned it into strips of fabric.

Some strips he tied together and wound like a sash to anchor the severed skirt to her waist. Others he wound around her greasy feet to protect them from dirt. She felt ridiculous, but knew that he'd done the best he could. She did not complain.

As promised, she rode Beulah. The mule grunted and heaved a mournful sigh. Angus shouldered another pack to relieve some of the animal's burden. They saw no one on the lonely road that day. Late that afternoon they entered Shipshead.

Angus stopped first at the Amherst Hotel, the town's largest hotel and saloon, to procure a room for the woman he was determined to make his. Persuaded by a gold nugget, the proprietor hastened to comply and, at the mountain man's urging, dispatched a whore to find clothes for the woman and summon the town's physician. The whore found her a dress and the physician dosed her with laudanum. Angelica soon fell into a drugged sleep while he treated her badly blistered feet.

"I got business to take care of," Angus said to the proprietor. "You make sure nothing bad happens to her."

The proprietor nodded and promised to keep her safe. "She's a fine piece, Goose. When you're finished with her, I'll offer her a job here. Lotta men go for women as purty as that. She'd have no trouble earnin' her keep, that's fer sure."

Straightening to his full, imposing height, Angus glowered at the man. "She ain't for sale. She's *respectable*."

"Sure, anything you say, Goose," the man placated.

Angus grunted and left. He sold the hides for a good price and dipped into his pouches of gold to buy himself new duds and pretty fripperies for his Angel. He stopped in at the general store to order things a woman might need, like an assortment of pots and pans and fine dishes and glassware. He bought a spool of lace, even if he didn't know what she'd do with it. It was fancy and feminine and, therefore, something he thought she deserved. He purchased flour and cornmeal and dried fruit and sugar and some precious spices, everything he saw that he thought a woman might like for the kitchen. And, because it was his Angel, he bought every new pack of cards the shop offered.

Maybe she'd consent to teach him some of those fancy card tricks. He decided that she'd for damn sure not have to rely on gambling ever again to support herself.

After bidding the shopkeeper to hold his purchases for delivery, he headed to the stagecoach office. Remembering the details of her ticket, he demanded the stagecoach company refund his Angel's money. The clerk at the ticket window refused and cowered behind the shelter of the iron bars shielding him from aggressive customers.

Angus tromped to the church and took hold of the preacher's arm. When that good man protested such rough treatment, he said, "I mean to get married and you're gonna do it."

"Goose!"

Angus ignored the man's blustering and dragged him into the hotel and up to the room where he'd carried the love of his life. He spluttered. She wasn't there.

"Where is she?" he bellowed.

The saloon's bouncer answered. "Your woman's fleecing our patrons, Goose. Better get her outta here before someone takes exception."

Livid, Angus rushed downstairs to the parlor to see Angelica dressed in a whore's finery, sporting dark circles under her eyes and handling the cards with uncanny skill. She laid down her hand, a full house of two aces and three queens, and declared, "My win, gentlemen."

"Fucking whore! You cheated!" a nattily dressed man accused as he jumped to his feet. His arm lashed out to strike the woman. She cringed to avoid the blow.

Angus caught the man's arm and bent it backward until the bone cracked and the man whimpered. "That's *my* woman you're insulting. She don't cheat. Now pay up and leave."

Color flagged her high cheekbones as Angelica gathered her winnings. Hot tears made her eyes shine at the protection the big man gave her. She looked at the men gathered around the table and thanked them for the game. The proprietor rose to his feet and stomped over to Angus.

"Goose, your woman just cleaned out the house!"

"How much do you owe her?" he asked.

"She's got the deed, damn her."

Angus gaped. *Damn, she really was good!* "Are you saying she now owns this here property?"

The proprietor nodded, looking sickly at the fact.

Angus looked back at Angelica who met his gaze without flinching, although he swore he saw shame in her eyes. He thought of everything he'd purchased for her and wondered if it were all a wasted expense.

"Angel, what are you gonna do with this place?"

"Mr. Amherst," she gestured toward the proprietor, "is welcome to stay on as the manager. I'll sit in on the card games and win for the house."

"I ain't working for no n—er—woman," Henry Amherst protested.

"Then you're out of a job," Angelica said, every syllable falling distinct and clear in the sudden quiet.

"You shouldn't have done that," Angus rumbled under his breath.

She held up the deed. "This gives me security."

He wanted to flinch at an insult he didn't think she knew she delivered. Softly, he said, "I can give you security."

Angelica did flinch at the softly spoken reproach. Still, she met his gaze with a courage few possessed. "I'm sorry, Angus. When I woke from my nap, you were nowhere to be found. I thought you'd left and I had to earn money for my keep."

That's plausible. Angus thought quickly. "You want to play cards?"

She sighed. Her elegant fingers twitched. "I think I *need* to play cards. It's in my blood, you know."

He nodded. She was Philippe Durand's daughter, after all. He glared at the property's former owner. "We'll be back at least once every month. Angel here will play cards if she wants to."

Henry gaped and his throat worked. Before he could utter a sound of objection, Angus turned to the preacher who was trying to sneak out.

"Preacher! You say the words here and now. You wed me to this woman!"

He wrapped his hand around his Angel's garishly clad arm, his grip light and unbreakable. The warmth of her skin met the heat of his palm. Angus thought his blood had begun to sizzle. A lovely flush rose from beneath the low cut bodice up the slender, elegant column of his woman's neck. He knew what that flush meant and it boded well for what he intended.

Angelica felt a quiver of excitement ripple through her body. *Not only kind, generous, and handsome, but commanding, too. A woman could do worse, much worse.*

The preacher flinched and minced his way toward the big man, pulling his pocket Bible from his black coat.

Angus glared at Henry. "When she marries me, everything she owns becomes mine. Then you'll be working for *me*, not her."

"At least you ain't no woman," Henry muttered.

Angelica's lips curved in a small, secret smile. *No, he's all man.*

"Well, that's okay then," Henry huffed with a curt nod.

"Orders from my Angel is the same as orders from me. Got it?"

Henry grunted. Angus took it for assent and prompted, "Preacher?"

The preacher opened his pocket Bible and quickly rattled off the marital vows. Three minutes later, Angus ordered the bouncer to gather up his wife's winnings and store them in the hotel safe.

"How much is there?" he asked Angelica.

"Four hundred thirteen dollars and twenty-two cents," she replied. "Plus the deed."

Angus glared at Henry. "One penny of that goes missing from the safe and I'll kill you."

Sweat beaded on Henry's upper lip and he nodded.

"The best suite here empty?" he asked.

Henry nodded and patted perspiration from his face with a handkerchief.

Angus grinned. "Good. I got a honeymoon to start."

Angelica yelped in surprise as he swung her into his arms and carried her up the stairs.

"Whatcha you gonna do with the saloon, wife?" he asked on the way up.

"It's your saloon," she replied, dark eyes sparkling.

"Nah, it's yours in every way that matters. You could rename it, 'cause it don't belong to Henry Amherst no more."

She smiled at him. "How about Aces High?"

Understanding the reference to what was usually a winning poker hand, he nuzzled her cheek and replied, "Nah. How about Angels High?"

The Mail Order Bride's Choice

Looking to improve her circumstances, an indigent woman travels across the country as a mail order bride to meet a fiancé who has plans for her other than marriage.

He hid so he could catch her in the act of returning a book to his father's library. He neither knew nor cared whether his father had granted her permission to borrow books from his library.

"I could have Mother dismiss you without a character reference for taking what doesn't belong to you," he commented as he emerged from concealment.

Moira gasped and, whirling around, nearly fell off the stepstool needed to reach the highest shelves. Face reddening with embarrassment and then turning pale as she understood her predicament, she carefully climbed down and faced her employer's entitled son.

"Your father granted me permission to read the books

as long as I returned them and reading did not interfere with my duties," she said. "'Twas most gracious of Mr. Swinburne."

"Gracious indeed, you little liar," young Mr. Swinburne sneered as he prowled closer.

Moira backed up, flattened her back against the bookshelves she herself had dusted the day before. "I'm no liar, sir. Ask Mr. Swinburne for the truth of it."

Young Mr. Swinburne chuckled, although the sound grated on her ears. "Who would have thought an Irish serving girl could read?"

"This is my half-day off," she reminded him. Bobbing a small curtsey, she added, "I'll be off now."

He reached out and gripped a shelf at her shoulder's height, barring the way.

"Oh, I don't think so, Moira. Now what will you give me to keep your employment?"

Since Moira had spent most of the past five years dodging the handsy young man and his rackety friends, all of whom felt themselves entitled to whatever female flesh they considered available, she knew what he wanted her to give him.

"I've done no wrong, Mr. Swinburne. Now, please allow me to go."

He lifted his other hand, traced a finger down the curve of her cheek and the slender column of her neck, hooking the tip beneath the high collar of her bodice. He tugged at the plain fabric, a hint of what he wanted to do, of what he might do.

"Oh, I don't think so, pretty Moira." He watched her face as her emotions congealed into fear mixed with resentment. He sighed. Bedding the recalcitrant beauty would require an exchange of money, money he preferred to spend on himself. "I'll settle you in a cozy apartment and buy you pretty dresses."

"I'm—"

"You trollop! Harlot!"

Both Moira and young Mr. Swinburne looked up at the horrified expression on his mother's face. Quivering with outrage, the woman hissed, "Get out! I knew you were working your evil wiles on my son, but—"

"Mrs. Swinburne, I did no such thing!" Moira protested.

"The evidence is right before my eyes, you Jezebel," the woman of the house snapped. She extended her hand toward her son. "Eugene, you mustn't let that gold digger sink her dirty claws into you. Come away from her, darling."

Summoned to his mother's side, Eugene Swinburne grinned at his prey. His gloating eyes held the promise of getting his way via an erroneous assumption that her need to earn an income ensured compliance. Whether she agreed to warm his bed while working as his family's maid or as his mistress, he assumed he knew her fate.

The maid took a step away from the bookshelves and squared her shoulders. She knew what was coming and she resolved to face it with her pride intact.

"You'll leave this house at once," Mrs. Swinburne snapped. "You'll receive no character reference from me and don't even think that you'll find respectable employment in this city again. I'll see you in the gutter where you belong."

Moira bobbed her last curtsey and replied, "Yes, ma'am."

Her hand wrapped around her son's upper arm, Mrs. Swinburne swept from the library, her son in tow and muttering deprecations against her obviously flawed decision to bring a pretty maid into the household.

"I should have known better than to exercise charity and kindness to that ungrateful girl. Bad blood will always tell."

Moira headed to the small attic room she shared with the Swinburnes' other maid. Caroline, who had the next Sunday afternoon off, likely toiled in the kitchen at that moment helping the cook prepare a lavish feast for that night's supper party. Moira collected her meager belongings, stuffing them into a worn satchel purchased secondhand and given to her by her mother five years prior. Mama had also given parting words of wisdom: "Stay true to yourself, Moira. Your virtue is all you truly possess. Give it to no man without the security of wedding vows."

Having grown up the bastard daughter of a tavern wench, Moira knew her mother spoke from harsh experience. A butler's daughter who had learned to read and write and expected to rise to respectable employment as some nobleman's housekeeper, Edith Saccarrigan had fallen for a nobleman's blandishments and false promises with the obvious consequences. Poor decisions and ruin followed her from Ireland to America. She gave her daughter the only gifts she could: advice and the skills to read and write.

Moira could still hear her mother's soft Irish brogue as she sang the sad, lilting songs of her homeland.

The Swinburne's butler met her at the back door—the servants entrance—with the salary owed her. He gave her a melancholy look and said, "You're a good worker, an honest girl. Should anyone inquire of me, I'll recommend your employment. I'm sorry, girl."

"I'm sorry, too," she replied. "You've been good to me, Mr. Conley."

He nodded and stepped back to allow her to pass through the doorway. Neither acknowledged that no one would ask the butler for his recommendation of a potential employee. Moira carried her belongings to the post office where she greeted the clerk and picked up the single letter waiting for her. Stepping aside and taking a seat on a public bench, she opened it. What good fortune! Her expression brightened as she picked up a ticket for the stagecoach from within the folds of paper.

Dear Miss Saccariggan,

Our amiable correspondence has convinced me that we will make a good life together. Please use the enclosed ticket to meet me in Redstone Falls in the Colorado Territory. I will greet you at the stagecoach depot and we'll marry.

Very truly yours,

Blake Garrison

Tucking the letter and ticket securely into her satchel, Moira left the post office and walked to the nearest stagecoach depot.

"When does the next stagecoach depart?" she inquired.

The clerk looked at the schedule posted on the wall beside the ticket window and replied, "Tomorrow morning, promptly at six o'clock."

Moira pursed her lips as she considered what to do next. She had little money to spend.

Raking his gaze over plain clothing, the clerk frowned and said, "You can't spend the night here, miss. The company don't allow passengers to loiter."

She sighed. The clerk obviously had experience with passengers like her.

"Do you know of an inexpensive place—someplace respectable—where I could stay for the night?" she asked.

He nodded. "Mrs. Tobymire keeps a lodging house on the corner of Williamson and Dutchman Streets. She'll feed you supper and breakfast, plain fare, but good. You might have to share accommodations with another female."

Moira nodded and thanked him. She gripped the handle of her satchel and hiked eleven blocks to the boarding house where she did indeed have to share a room with another woman who happened to be scheduled to ride the same stagecoach for the same purpose. That was all right, because both women were accustomed to sharing bed space—Moira with another maid, Suzanne with her younger sister.

As promised, Mrs. Tobymire included hearty, plain fare with payment for the night's lodging. The fierce looking woman effectively discouraged any illicit shenanigans from the rowdier patrons.

The bed smelled of the sweat and dirt of other patrons, testifying that Mrs. Tobymire laundered the sheets on a schedule, not between guests. However, Moira ignored that, bolstered by the knowledge that she would meet and wed the kind and generous Blake Garrison in just a few short weeks.

The next morning after washing their faces and hands and gobbling down a heavy breakfast of oatmeal, eggs, rolls leftover from the night before, and coffee, the young women kept each other company on the walk to the depot.

"Load up!" the stagecoach driver shouted minutes after they arrived.

Moira and Suzanne climbed in after handing their baggage to the shotgun messenger. They squeezed in beside an elderly couple and two large, bearded men stinking of the previous night's revelry. The vehicle jiggled as four restive horses danced in the traces.

"Hi-yah!" the coachman bellowed and cracked his whip. The four horses launched into a fast trot that could be sustained for only a few miles after which both horses and passengers would walk before the horses had rested sufficiently to pick the pace back up again. The leather struts beneath the passenger enclosure caused a rocking motion that the elderly gentleman assured the young women was preferable to those coaches featuring steel springs.

"Rocking is better than bouncing," he concluded with a nod.

Mile after punishing mile with stops every few hours at stations along the way to change exhausted teams for fresh horses, the six passengers had little to do but converse. Soon, everyone knew everyone else's life story. The elderly couple traveled west to live with their youngest daughter and her family. The two bearded men intended to make their fortunes mining silver or copper in the Rocky Mountains.

One of the bearded men made overtures at the young women, despite them informing him they were engaged to be married, until his friend swatted him and said, "Henry, the girls ain't interested. Leave 'em alone."

With ill grace, Henry subsided. Both Moira and Suzanne heaved sighs of relief.

Moira once thought covering nearly 2,000 miles in just under six weeks as miraculous and speedy, but the long, hard days of feeling like a sardine wedged among the other passengers quickly relieved her of the romance of travel. Despite discomfort, poorly cooked and sometimes rancid food, lower than usual standards of hygiene, and mile after mile of mud or alkali dust, the passengers gave thanks when they arrived unmolested by stagecoach robbers or hostile Indians. Delays due to torrential rains, two broken wheels, a broken axle, and one passenger's illness requiring a physician's attention, brought them into town much later than expected.

Disembarking from the cramped vehicle, Moira and Suzanne looked about for the gentlemen who pledged to meet them. They saw no one.

"Whom are you meeting?" Suzanne inquired.

"Mr. Blake Garrison," Moira replied as she peered into the dusty darkness. Rain and mud had delayed their arrival and she feared her fiancé had not waited.

"No, *I'm* meeting Blake Garrison," the pretty brunette

said. "You must be meeting someone else."

"No, I—" Moira dug into her satchel and pulled out the letter. She presented it to Suzanne. "Here, read it. My intended is Blake Garrison."

Suzanne scanned the missive and, jaw dropping in astonishment, pulled out her letter for comparison. Moira frowned as she recognized the handwriting, read the sweet words she had memorized over a month ago. Looking up at her friend, she stated the obvious, "We've been brought out here under false pretenses."

"But why?" the other woman blurted as Moira handed the letter back.

Moira shook her head at the other girl's naiveté and said, "For no good purpose, I'm sure."

"What shall we do?" the young woman wailed.

"We shall seek the assistance of the local sheriff or pastor," Moira decided. She hoped local law enforcement would not require the victims of this deceit repay their fare.

She tightened her grip on the handle of her satchel and linked arms with her friend. "We'd best be going before Mr. Garrison shows up and demands repayment for our stagecoach fares."

Lips pressed together in a thin line of determination, Suzanne nodded and set a brisk pace. The depot had closed for the night, so no clerk remained from whom they could ask directions. They picked a direction by flipping a penny: heads for east, tails for west. They headed west, walking along the boardwalk which saved pedestrians from the worst of the mud splatter from horses and carriages traveling the unpaved main street. At that late hour, the street was largely deserted. As they neared the end of the street, they crossed in front of a saloon. Badly played piano music, raucous laughter, and coarse words wafted on the smoky air that flowed above and below the batwings.

"Hey, Blake, when's them new girls gettin' in?" someone shouted, then belched just as loudly. "We're hankerin' for some fresh meat."

"The stagecoach was delayed, Ruben. I'll pick 'em up tomorrow, then put 'em to work repaying their fare."

"Oh, dear," Suzanne gasped as realization set in. "He means us."

Moira felt the young woman tremble and wanted to join her. Instead, she swung her around and changed direction.

"West wasn't a good choice," she murmured. "Let's try east."

They crossed the muddy street and headed in the opposite direction until they finally found the sheriff's office. The golden glow of a single candle alerted them to the presence of a lawman. With a polite knock on the door, the young women summoned their courage and entered.

A lanky man reclined in a hard chair, feet propped on the desk, head tipped back. He snored. Loudly.

"Ahem!" Moira cleared her throat to get his attention. The man continued snoring. In a much louder tone, she barked, "Sheriff!"

"What? Huh?" The man woke with a snort and reached for his pistol. Squinting his bloodshot eyes, he set the pistol aside and glared at the intruders. "Who are you and what do you want?"

Suzanne opened her mouth, but a warning clench of Moira's hand on hers stopped the words from pouring out.

"Are you the sheriff, sir?" Moira asked.

"Deputy. Now I'll repeat my question: who are you and what do you want?"

"We'd really prefer to speak with the sheriff," Moira insisted.

"Sheriff's chasing down an outlaw, so all's you get is me."

Moira sighed and explained their circumstances as

tersely as she could.

"That damned flesh monger," the deputy growled, eyes narrowing as he looked upon the two pretty women who had nowhere to go and no one but him to help them. He sighed. Women—the kind a man married—were in short supply and high demand in Redstone Falls. They'd land on their feet soon enough. In the meantime, he felt obligated to escort them to the church. The brunette caught his eye, but his own wife would skin him alive if he brought that one home.

"Pastor Levy's missus sometimes takes in strays for a little extra income," he explained on the way. "She'll give ya a cot and a hot."

Both young women blinked at the lingo and took a moment to translate it.

"We're grateful, Deputy," Suzanne replied. Moira nodded.

He took them around the back of the white clapboard church to the parsonage. He rapped on the door. A short, squat woman answered, her bushy eyebrows meeting in a frown of disapproval.

"Deputy, what's going on?"

"I got two young ladies what was lured here under false pretenses by that snake, Blake Garrett. They need a place to stay for the night."

"I don't take in no whores, Deputy. You know that."

"They ain't whores, ma'am. They look like honest girls who was duped into coming out here to marry. I'm sure Pastor Levy will know some upstanding bachelors who'll be happy to get 'em off'n yer hands."

"Stupid mail order brides," the woman grumbled. She stepped back, raked her sharp gaze over the two young women and muttered, "Lads'll be frothing at the mouth for these girls." With a gesture, she ushered Moira and Suzanne inside. "Well, come on in, girls. I ain't gonna wait here all night."

The deputy nodded reassurance and the two young women entered. The door closed behind them, plunging the parsonage into darkness dimly illuminated by the light of one lantern.

"Follow me, girls. I got one room for you. You'll have to share the bed."

The young women followed, grateful to have a safe place to lie down.

"Seein' as you were lied to," Mrs. Levy said, "I'll cut my usual rate in half for the accommodations tonight, just four bits each. That includes a fresh pitcher of wash water tomorrow morning and breakfast. There's a pitcher of water in the room right now for you to use. You're responsible for emptying the basin in the morning. You want to stay longer, it'll be a dollar each per night."

Having no better option, Moira and Suzanne nodded in agreement. After performing their evening ablutions, they climbed into bed and slept until dawn the next morning when a sharp knock woke them.

"Girls, get yer lazy selves downstairs. Breakfast is ready."

"The milk of human kindness runs like a river through this church," Moira commented under her breath.

Suzanne giggled at the sarcasm.

Hastily dressed, they joined the pastor and his wife at the table. An Indian squaw with a disgruntled expression served them. The food was surprisingly good and plentiful.

"What do we do now?" Suzanne asked, looking to her friend for inspiration as they stood on the stoop, baggage in hand. The parsonage door slammed shut behind them.

Moira sighed, then answered, "Let's head for the mercantile. Perhaps the proprietor will know where we can find work."

Suzanne snorted. "If I wanted to work for a living, I wouldn't have signed up as a mail order bride."

"Women do nothing but work," Moira retorted. "But

being a wife's supposed to offer stability."

Suzanne shrugged.

They found the general store. One of the patrons grinned as he saw what entered. Approaching them, he asked, "Well, hello, ladies, what can I do for you?"

Moira distrusted the avaricious gleam in the man's eye and, once again, spoke for herself and Suzanne. "We'd like to speak with the proprietor of this establishment. Would you direct us, please?"

A large, prosperous looking man behind the counter turned to face them. His eyes widened and he wiped his hands down the front of the apron he wore to protect his clothes. "I'm Stan Larrimar and I own this here store. May I help you ladies?"

"Stan, we need to settle this," the customer at the counter complained without turning around.

The shopkeeper waved his hand. "You'll hold, Callum. These pretty ladies won't. Now, ladies, what can I do to—er—*for* you?"

Suzanne's eyes gleamed and she donned her most charming smile as she approached the shopkeeper. "We arrived on the stagecoach yesterday evening. We're—"

Moira interrupted. "Sir, we're seeking work, respectable work."

The shopkeeper chuckled. "The only respectable *work* you girls is gonna find is marriage." His gaze focused on the petite brunette. "I do like me a pretty handful like yerself." He spread his arms wide to indicate his wealth. "You object to bein' a merchant's wife?"

"Ah, hell," the man at the counter groaned under his breath. "Just 'cause Sally Mae Jessup rejected your suit to be a rancher's wife ..."

Suzanne smiled at the shopkeeper and seized the opportunity. She took a deep breath to draw his attention to her plump bosom. "No, sir. I'm quite good with sums and can help you manage the store."

Stan untied his apron and whipped it off. Tossing it behind him with a triumphant laugh, he came from around the counter and offered Suzanne his arm. She rested her hand in the crook of his elbow. Looking back at his customers, the shopkeeper shouted, "Boys, I'll be back shortly. I got me a *bride*! Callum, you go ahead and sign that contract."

"Ah, hell," the man at the counter muttered again.

Moira blinked, astonished that her friend would leave her behind so readily. She blinked again, realizing that she still had to sort out her own situation.

The satchel dragged at her arm, which felt as though it might separate from her shoulder. She crossed the wooden floor and heaved her bag to the countertop where the other man leaned over some papers. The bag didn't quite make it.

"Easy there, little lady," the man said as he caught the bag with effortless strength and set it atop the counter. He took a look at her weary expression of dismay and offered her a stick of horehound candy. "You look like you could use this."

"Oh, I couldn't possibly accept." She desperately wanted that sweetness in her mouth, but knew she couldn't afford the cost even at a penny per dozen.

He shrugged. "It's just a piece of candy, ma'am. A gift with no strings attached."

Moira's eyes welled with tears at the small, simple kindness. She accepted the candy and stuck it in her mouth. She sighed as the sugary treat began to melt on her tongue. It had been so long since she'd enjoyed something so much.

Callum Argent's eyes bugged and he damn near groaned as those plump, rosy lips surrounded that lucky stick of candy. Her sigh of appreciation made other parts of him perk up, too. He almost thought he heard his mother's voice whisper in his ear, *Don't let this one go, boy. I sent her here for you.*

From behind them came an offer. "You know, miss, you could come *work* for me. I c'n always use another blonde."

Callum snorted. "Leave her be, Billy. She don't want to be no whore."

"Well, I ain't lookin' to get married just yet." Billy turned his attention back to Moira, his gaze running over her with a familiarity that made her squirm. "I'd make it real good for ya, better money than Garrison. He's a cheap son of a bitch."

"Watch your mouth, Billy," Callum said at the same time Moira took the candy from her mouth and replied in a tone so frosty that snow could have fallen from the ceiling. "No, thank you."

The man adjusted the brim of his hat and sniffed. "Iff'n you find yerself still lookin' for *employment*, you come on down to the Silver Spur Saloon and I'll put ya to work."

"Go away, Billy," Callum said. He turned toward the tired woman standing stiffly beside him, face red with shame or embarrassment. He didn't know which and knew it didn't matter. "Ma'am, my name's Callum, Callum Argent, foreman out at the Triple D. Mr. Denney's been lookin' for someone to teach his young'uns how to read and cipher, if yer interested."

"I'm not qualified to be a governess," Moira replied, shoulders drooping. She glanced at the papers in front of Callum.

Billy took his leave and the door slammed shut behind him.

"You sure talk like one o' them fancy school teachers from back east."

She gave him a wry smile and said nothing. Her gaze dropped back to those papers, curiosity getting the better of her.

"You read, ma'am?"

"Yes, I do," she admitted.

"You think maybe you could help me with this?" he asked, pointing at the papers.

"I can try," she replied.

He nodded and took a step back. "Read 'em and tell me what you think."

She stuck the candy back in her mouth and nodded. She thought that Callum might have groaned softly as her lips closed over the stick, but couldn't be sure. Focusing her attention on the papers, she read through them, then riffled them together in a neat stack.

"What do you think?"

Reading Mr. Swinburne's business and history books kept my mind sharp, she thought. *Let's hope Mr. Argent appreciates it.* She took a deep breath, removed the candy from her mouth, and replied, "I think someone's trying to cheat you."

He nodded, expression darkening even as he focused on those plump, rosy lips and wondered what they'd taste like. "That's what I thought, too."

Moira pointed to a paragraph on the second page. "You see, Mr. Argent, this says that you're not actually buying the land, but merely leasing it. This clause states the property owner has a lawful claim on any crops you raise or on any proceeds from the sale of your crops in addition to fees paid to lease the property."

"You're a smart lady," Callum said, eyes brightening with appreciation not only for her blonde beauty but also her sharp mind. His body tightened as she took another deep breath. He took a deep breath, too, nostrils flaring at the warm, sweet scent of womanly flesh. He hardly recognized the urge to offer her everything he possessed just to see her smile at him with favor. *I've spent too long among dirty, stinky wranglers and cattle.* "Anything else tip you off?"

She frowned in concentration for a few seconds, then flipped to the third page. "See here—" she pointed "—the terms of the lease state that you agree to a ten percent increase in lease fees every year. That's what *per annum* means."

Callum blinked and deadly anger simmered in his gut. "No wonder Stan was pressin' me to sign."

"Oh, he wasn't helping you analyze the contract?"

He met her big, blue eyes that blinked in astonished comprehension. His lips curled in an embarrassed smile. "No ma'am, I can't read. He wrote the contract and was supposed to be tellin' me what it said."

She frowned in anger on his behalf. "That's outrageous! He's trying to swindle you!"

"So it seems," Callum agreed. "Well, now that I've got you on my side, how about you and me discuss you and me."

Moira looked into his intelligent brown eyes beneath the wide brim of his hat. Dark brown curls stuck out beneath the hat and a thick brown mustache stretched across his upper lip. She took another deep breath and inhaled the smells of sunshine, dust, and male musk mingled with the faint, underlying odor of horse sweat.

"It ... it wouldn't be appropriate," she forced herself to say when all she wanted to do was lean on this man's kindness and strength. *Just once, I'd like to rely on someone other than myself.*

"You came out here to be married, right?" he gently prodded.

She nodded and averted her eyes, ashamed of how she'd been duped.

Feeling bold, he took her gloved hand in his. "Ma'am ... miss ... truth is, there ain't no respectable work out here for a respectable woman. Men outnumber women here by a lot, and most won't care none whether you're willin' before draggin' you off."

He shrugged one broad shoulder. "We got two saloons with about a dozen whores between 'em. They ain't ... *suf-*

ficient ... for this town and that mining camp nearby. Men here are on edge, if you know what I mean."

"And you?" she queried with suspicion.

He gave her a closed-mouth smile and a curt nod of acknowledgement before answering. "I'm a little pickier than most. 'Sides, my mama would blister my hide if I hurt a woman."

"And is your mother near?"

"Mama's in heaven where the angels do her bidding and even God asks for her permission before handing out miracles."

Moira ignored the blasphemy and smiled at the ring of truth in his voice. "She sounds formidable."

"That's the truth. She managed me, pa, and my nine brothers with an iron hand. There weren't nobody tougher than my mama." He held out his arm and gave her an honest smile, strong white teeth gleaming against tanned skin. She noticed that he had all his teeth and they were mostly straight. Callum saw the longing in her eyes and how her dress hung loosely on her already slender body. "How about I treat you to lunch? You look as if you've been missing meals."

The woman who fascinated him still held back, so he tried additional persuasion by appealing to her sense of propriety.

"Maisie Dellacroix's place is just down the street. She's from New Orleans and serves food with funny names, but tastes so good yer tongue will slap your brain." He watched her resolve soften, but not quite enough, so he added, "We'll be with other folks, not alone."

That reassurance almost made her yank her hand away and race out the door, because what could one man do against a town full of men hungry for women any way they could get them? A keen horseman and sharp foreman, Callum read the woman's expression and body language and understood her renewed reluctance.

"You're perfectly safe with me. I'll protect you, Miss ... Miss ..."

"Moira Saccariggan," the pretty blonde answered, tucking a stray lock of yellow hair behind her ear. She took another deep breath and summoned her courage. "Yes, Mr. Argent, I'd enjoy having lunch with you. Thank you."

Callum grinned. He picked up a pen and pulled the ink-well closer. Handing her the pen, he asked, "Before we go, would you mind striking out those unfair terms?"

"Of course," she replied and ran lines of ink through the offensive clauses. Handing the pen back to him, she advised, "I suggest you not sign it as of yet."

"No worry, I won't. I just want Stan to know that I'm not an idiot."

"I don't think you're an idiot," she murmured. In a moment of self-loathing, she reserved that appellation for herself. She crunched off the end of the stick of candy, wrapped the remainder in a bit of paper torn from the last page of the contract, and tucked it into a pocket to save for later. She hoped it wouldn't stick.

He offered his arm and she rested her hand on it. He took her bag in his other hand, carrying it for her. They left the store as Stan swept his newly wed bride off her feet to carry her in.

"Did you sign that contract, Callum?"

"It's on the countertop."

"Good. I'll get back to you soon. I got me a *wife*."

Suzanne's giggle floated back to them as the shop-keeper hurried inside to take his bride to his bed. Moira sighed.

"What's wrong, Miss Saccariggan?"

"I just thought she'd be smarter after having been so recently duped."

Callum shrugged. "Stan's a greedy businessman, but I don't think he'd treat his woman badly. He was always good to his mama and sister, even after their pa died."

That's a relief. "What do you think will happen now?"

Callum chuckled. "Well, if all goes according to Stan's plan, he'll be a father in nine months and bring up his son to follow in his footsteps."

Moira huffed in feigned offense. The man had a devilish sense of humor and needed to be kept in line. She rather thought she might enjoy that task.

"That's not what I meant."

"Then what did you mean?" he asked, knowing very well what she meant. She looked into his twinkling eyes and huffed again. He laughed and said, "All right, here's what's gonna happen. We're gonna have us a nice lunch. Then we're gonna head to the church. And then we're gonna get married."

Heat flooded his body as those last two sentences rolled off his tongue without his permission. He felt his body tighten; the fit of his britches grew snug.

"You don't know anything about me," Moira protested in shock. "How can you want to marry me?"

They stopped on the boardwalk, and he trapped her close to a building's outer wall with the nearness of his own body. Drawing her closer to him and ignoring the curious stares of passersby, Callum answered: "You're the prettiest thing I've ever seen. I can tell you're kind, brave, and strong, because you tried to protect the new Mrs. Larrimar. And you're smart. You're everything I've ever wanted in a woman. Marry me. I vow to protect you and give you the best life I can. Accept me, and I'll praise the good Lord every day for listening to my mama."

Moira took another deep breath of spring air scented with mud, rain, the tang of pine, and clean male musk. She looked into eyes that sparkled with good humor, kindness, and intelligence. She let her gaze rove down his body: tall, lean, broad shoulders, narrow waist. Sensing the far-reaching repercussions of her decision, she still hesitated.

"I'm buying my own spread," he said, sweetening his

offer and knowing what security meant to a woman who had none. "It won't be an easy life, but we'll make it a good one."

She looked down at the toes of her worn shoes poking from beneath threadbare skirts. Did she dare turn her future over to this handsome stranger?

Callum sighed. "Look, I understand why you'd not want to shackle yourself to me. I'm a stranger. You don't know me. Just ... just give me a chance to court you."

She looked back up at him and nearly flinched at his earnest expression. She lifted her other hand and pressed the gloved palm over his heart. She felt the fast, heavy thump and knew he was as nervous as she. Moira held her silence and almost thought she heard another woman's voice whisper in her ear, *He's what you need. Accept him and be happy.*

"I always thought I'd marry for love," she whispered more to herself than him.

"Then why'd you come to Redstone Falls as a mail order bride?" he countered.

She sighed at his logic and smiled with sudden decision. "So I could meet you."

Two hours later after Pastor Levy performed his second impromptu wedding ceremony of the day, Mrs. Levy was heard to mutter, "I knew them girls would get snapped up fast. Too bad, though. I'da liked to earn another coupla dollars off 'em."

When Blake Garrison heard that he missed the arrival of the two young ladies he'd lured to Redstone Falls under false pretenses and that they'd married, he howled in outrage at having lost the money spent on their fare and the future income they would have brought him. No one empathized, least of all Billy, who owned the other saloon on the east end of town.

Coming Home

Life is hard. No one knows this better than Dessie Humphrey who's trying to hold onto the family farm. When aid comes in the form of a wanted gunslinger, she's in no position to refuse.

There was a reason gravediggers were men. They had greater strength and could dig faster and deeper than any woman. Desdemona Ophelia Antoinette Humphrey—so named by her late mother, unlamented for saddling her with such a cumbersome name—wiped her sweaty forehead with the back of a dirty sleeve before shoveling the last few spades of dirt on her father's grave. The milk cow lowed in the barn and the horses neighed from the corral, reminding her that they were hungry.

"I'm hungry, too," she muttered to no one in particular and silently promised to say a few prayers over Papa's grave the next morning. She still had work to do.

With a sigh, Dessie tamped the dirt and then dragged the shovel behind her on the way to the barn. She fed the horses first, then returned to the barn and fed the cow.

The usually placid beast munched hay as she grabbed the milk bucket and a stool. After taking a moment to crack her knuckles, Dessie set herself to the task of milking the cow.

When the pail was full, she carried it into the house and set it on the countertop. The cat meowed, wanting her share of the warm, creamy liquid.

"Here you go, Faust," she said, pouring him a small dish and setting it on the floor. Sighing, she straightened and groaned as stiffening muscles protested. She looked about the small cabin, two days of chores undone because she'd had to tend to her father's body.

Damn him for leaving her all alone.

Dessie chastised herself under her breath for such uncharitable thoughts. Papa did the best he could. It wasn't his fault he'd been gored by that bull. It wasn't his fault the wound had festered. It wasn't … *Oh, yes, it was. I told him not to mess with that bull, but, no, he wouldn't listen to me.*

Her very bones ached with exhaustion, yet there'd be no supper if she did not cook it. She'd eaten the last of the bread the day before. Her eyes watered with self-pity as she hauled in a bucket of water to fill the kettle. After putting the kettle on the hearth to boil, she fetched the last few logs from the wood pile and added them to the coals. If she were lucky, the coals remained hot enough to ignite the wood. She wasn't. So, she fetched some kindling and nursed the coals into igniting the kindling which then did their job by giving the logs enough time to catch fire.

She scooped out the last of the flour, made a basic dough with two eggs gathered from the hens that morning, a generous spoonful of bicarbonate of soda, and a splash of milk.

"I think we have some cheese left," she muttered to herself and the cat, but found none. "Damn."

She smiled, though the expression was bitter. She repeated the profanity a little louder. That felt good. Liberating.

She added more milk to the dough and kneaded it until the sponge felt elastic. Dessie plopped the dough into a Dutch oven and set it into the coals to bake. She'd have soda bread, fried eggs, and milk for supper. While the bread baked, she poured the remainder of the milk into the butter churn and began moving the paddle to make good use of the cow's contribution to the household before the milk spoiled in the summer heat.

By the time she went to bed, Dessie was almost too tired to wash. However, her mother's admonition of cleanliness being next to godliness mandated she expend the last of her energy fetching another pail of water and making good use of that. Respectable ladies did not retire for the night stinking like a stevedore.

Dessie's last thought as she closed her eyes was that she had no idea what a stevedore was.

The merry chirp of birds mingled with barnyard noises of hungry animals woke her the next morning. Dessie regarded the soiled dress she'd worn the day before with distaste and decided to wear her other dress. Possessing a sum total of three dresses, all in various states of threadbare deterioration, she donned the one clean gown that remained. As had become her custom, she took care of the livestock before feeding herself.

The sun rose, sending down muggy heat and light that shimmered over the hard-baked earth. With a small leather pouch of coins and the deed to the farm tucked into a pocket, she hitched the team of horses to Pa's old wagon and drove into town. She kept the horses at a plodding walk, so the journey took nearly two hours.

After tying the team at a water trough, Dessie headed for the office of the town's only attorney.

"Well, Miss Humphrey, what brings you here today?" Donald Ostwich, Esq. inquired as he smoothed back his shiny, pomaded hair.

"Papa died," she replied with blunt candor. Dessie was

too doggone tired to fool with idle pleasantries and chit-chat. She pulled the deed from her pocket and held it up. "I need to transfer the farm into my name."

The attorney rubbed his clean-shaven chin. "Well, now, Miss Humphrey, that might be a bit of a problem."

"How so?"

"Well, legally, a woman can't own real property, unless she's a widow."

"Papa didn't have any sons and there are no male relations," she pointed out. "That leaves one descendant, one relation: me. I've got every right to inherit."

His eyes gleamed with an interest Dessie distrusted.

"Now, you know, Miss Humphrey, that I'll look into the matter for you. However, you should know that we could resolve this right quick if you were married. Do you have a beau?"

Dessie blinked, then looked over the man, gaze running from his lacquered hair over his protruding belly to his shiny shoes. His soft hands looked as though they'd never seen manual labor. She supposed a woman could do worse than hitch herself to that cart, but the idea of sharing a home and bed with him made her stomach churn.

Determined to be polite, she replied, "The farm is mine, Mr. Ostwich. Make it legal."

"Miss Humph—" he called after her, but she did not tarry. He grumbled to himself about the insolence of uppity misses. Surely, he could do better than one work-worn woman who hadn't any couth, regardless of the valuable property she inherited.

Gossip spread like wildfire through town, bringing a pack of hungry bachelors to Dessie Humphrey's door over the next few weeks. Since she labored in the fields and kitchen garden, she missed most of them. Those who weren't too lazy to search for her found her hard at work. She dismissed them all with a sharp word and the steady aim of Pa's pistol. Even a bad shot was a credible threat at close range.

"Ma'am?"

Hunched over as she weeded a row of carrots, Dessie leaned back on her heels and wiped the sweat from her forehead with the back of her sleeve. With a sigh, she turned to look at a man silhouetted against the afternoon sky. She took in what details she could: tall, broad shoulders, narrow waist, long legs. He wore a pistol at each hip. Cautious, because she did not recognize this stranger, Dessie slid one hand into her pocket for the heavy pistol she'd begun to carry when her suitors didn't want to take no for an answer.

"I'm not interested," she replied, blinking against the sun.

"I ain't sellin'."

"Then why are you here?"

"I heard tell there was a woman lookin' to manage her daddy's farm all by herself and thought I'd see if she needed some assistance."

Dessie pressed her lips together in a thin line. With her free hand, she waved to indicate her property. "I do, but I'm not looking to marry anyone just to get a helping hand."

The man's white teeth flashed beneath the lowered brim of his hat. "I ain't lookin' to get married, ma'am. I'm lookin' for paid work."

Dessie chewed on her bottom lip as she considered this new development. She most certainly could use a strong back and extra pair of hands, but she was short on resources. She decided to be honest with him.

"I don't have much money, mister, but I can offer you a place to stay in the barn and three meals a day. You take care of the livestock and crops; I'll take care of the house, chickens, and garden." The cow in the barn lowed. She sighed and added, "And I'll milk the cow."

"And laundry," the man added. "Add laundry and I'll

start this afternoon."

She frowned, then decided to compromise. "I'll wash your dirty clothes with mine, but I won't be washing extra loads just for you."

"Fair enough, ma'am."

She rose to her feet, grunting as her knees protested, and held out her hand. "Do we have an agreement, mister?"

He took her hand and shook it. His palm was dry and dusty. He nodded and replied, "Yes, ma'am, we do."

Dessie gestured toward the barn. "If you have a horse, you can stable it there. I've got some extra stalls available. Then pick up a sickle and head behind the barn. You'll see a field of winter wheat. It needs harvesting."

"Yes, ma'am."

"Call me Dessie. What should I call you?"

"John, John McClintock."

She nodded at him and watched as he walked away from her, noticing the bow in his legs indicating a life spent in the saddle. She wondered just what she had welcomed into her life and hoped she hadn't just made the biggest mistake ever.

"You're too trusting, Desdemona Ophelia Antoinette Humphrey," she muttered under her breath.

She looked up at the sound of hooves to see her new farmhand leading an obviously tired horse into the barn. Sinking back down onto her knees, she returned her attention to those pesky weeds, peeking up every so often. John McClintock emerged from the barn with a sickle, the cutting edge gleaming in the sun. She hummed to herself, realizing he'd taken the time to run a whetstone over the blade.

Dessie finished weeding the garden and harvested enough vegetables to make for supper that night. She had no meat and no inclination to slaughter one of her few precious laying hens. She hoped that John would be satisfied with a meal of bread, cheese, eggs, and vegetables. He wasn't. But all he said was, "I'll see if I can't shoot a couple rabbits or a goose for you tomorrow."

"Thank you. I'd appreciate that," she replied. "I set a basket outside the back door. Just dump your dirty laundry in that."

"Thank you, ma'am."

She handed him a blanket and bade him goodnight. John took the hint without demur and left. She barred the doors behind him.

The next morning, she rose at dawn. First she milked the cow, then fried some eggs, boiled some oatmeal, and brewed a pot of coffee. By the time John had fed and watered the livestock, she had breakfast ready.

"You want me to finish the wheat field today?" he asked as they ate.

"Yes, please. Stack the wheat in the wagon and I'll drive it into town. The mill has a threshing machine."

He nodded, thanked her for breakfast, and headed out. Dessie washed laundry that day.

They soon fell into a routine of hard labor punctuated by hot meals. They talked during those meals. Dessie told him of the pretty education her mother gave her and the fancy literature she read and the way her pa died. John spoke of the places he traveled, some of the men he'd known, and of his service in the war. She gave him her father's boots and he whittled fanciful figurines that she set on the mantle. A tentative alliance built of mutual need grew into a deep friendship based on trust and liking.

Over the next several weeks as midsummer marched toward autumn, John shot some deer and several geese and rabbits. He butchered the carcasses and Dessie hung them in the smokehouse to preserve the meat. She canned and dried what the garden produced, made butter and cheese, and sold what she could in town. When the evenings turned chill, she invited him to move into the small house.

"You can take Pa's bed," she said, gesturing toward the curtained-off alcove that had served as her father's bed-room.

Donald Ostwich, Esq. finally relented and signed over the transfer of the farm from her father's name, muttering against the idiocy of allowing women to own property.

"You need a husband, Miss Humphrey. A woman isn't suited to the responsibility of owning property. Allow me—"

"No, thank you, Mr. Ostwich," she interrupted. "I'm managing just fine."

After leaving the attorney's office, she stopped at the general store.

"How do, Miss Humphrey?" the proprietor greeted her.

"Fine, thank you, Mr. Rogers." She made her way to the section of the store where bolts of fabric were stored. "Have you any chambray?"

The man smiled. "Just got in a bolt last week. Would you like to see it?"

"I'll need three—no, make that four yards," she said, thinking that the poorly mended, threadbare condition of John's shirts was worse than her own worn clothing. She'd sew him a couple of new shirts.

Mr. Rogers looked puzzled. "Four yards ain't enough for a lady's dress and too much for a lady's shirt. Who're you sewing for?"

Lifting her chin in steely dignity, she said, "I hired a farmhand and he's in dire need of decent clothing."

The shopkeeper's eyes narrowed. "We haven't seen anybody new in town in months." He dug behind the counter and pulled out a wanted poster. "Your new farm-hand don't look like this man, does he?"

"Of course not," she replied, barely glancing at the drawing.

"Well, Miss Humphrey, if you see this man, you let the

sheriff know right away. He's dangerous, a notorious gun-slinger."

"Of course," she replied and cleared her throat. "My chambray?"

"Oh, yes. Would you like buttons and thread, too?"

"Please."

Dessie paid for her purchases with the money earned from selling butter, cheese, and eggs, then returned home. She said nothing until they sat down to supper.

"I saw your face on a wanted poster," she announced and fixed him with a look of disappointment.

John set down his knife and fork and leaned back in the chair. He exhaled through his mouth. "I'll pack up and leave tonight, Dessie."

"What did you do, John?" she asked.

"I killed a man, several men, actually."

"Did you murder them?"

"They drew first." *Sometimes*. He paused and ran a hand through his dark hair. "I'm a bounty hunter. Got tired of it, the constant wandering, the killing." He looked around the cabin. "I feel like I've put down roots here. It's comforting. This is *home*."

She nodded because she understood, even though she'd never killed a man nor traveled more than twenty miles from the farm. "John, you've dealt honestly with me and I'll do the same with you. Give me your word that you'll do me no harm—and, indeed, intend me no harm—and I'll keep your presence here a secret. I sorely need your help on the farm and it's nice to have company."

He nodded. The man's rigid shoulders relaxed, the only sign of his relief.

She said nothing more on the matter. Autumn brought the hectic schedule of getting the harvest in before the frost hit and planting next summer's crop of winter wheat. They worked long, grueling hours, Dessie often laboring beside John in the field. When she presented him with the shirt she made for him using one of his old shirts as a pattern, he blinked away suspicious wetness from his eyes as he murmured his gratitude. He couldn't remember the last time someone gave him a gift.

"Excuse me," he murmured and left before she could actually excuse him. When he returned minutes later, he dropped some gold coins into her hand.

"What's this?" she asked.

"Gold dollars," he said, mouth curling in a smirk.

"Well, I know that. I mean, what's this for? You've no need to repay me for the shirts."

"Consider it a gift," he said. "Buy yourself a pretty dress or three. You deserve them." *You need them.*

She looked down at the worn, mended fabric of her skirt and returned a rueful smile. "All right. My wardrobe could use refurbishing."

She paused, then asked, "Where are you keeping that money?"

His expression closed, turned cold. Before he could blister her with a harsh reply, she blurted, "I'm not after your money, John. It's just that it's not safe if you're keeping it in the barn."

"It's not safe if I keep it in the house," he said.

"I wouldn't steal from you!"

He gave her a sad little smile. "No, I trust in your honesty, Dessie. But anyone else searching for the money will look in the house. And it's not in the barn, either."

"Oh."

She did not ask again where he kept his stash of coins.

Finally, he asked a question that had irked him since he met her. "Dessie's an unusual name. Is it short for something?"

She sighed, her lips twisting in a wry smile an instant before burdening him with the full weight of her name. His eyebrows rose.

"That's a mouthful."

"Tell me about it."

They chuckled in harmony at her mother's grandiose notions and retired for the evening, John promising that he would milk the cow, feed the hens, and collect the eggs so Dessie could get an early start on the journey to town.

The long drive offered an opportunity for relaxation that did not often come Dessie's way. She enjoyed every minute of the relatively quiet trip with naught but singing birds, buzzing insects, and the noises of horses, harnesses, and a creaky wagon to disturb her peace. She fancied those gold coins burned a hole in her pocket. Ever mindful of the necessity of commerce, she hauled butter, cheese, and a basket of eggs to sell.

With his usual good cheer, Mr. Rogers greeted her and purchased the products she brought.

"How's that new farmhand working out, Miss Humphrey?" he inquired as he carefully transferred the eggs from her basket to his.

"Just fine, Mr. Rogers. He's a hard worker and polite. I couldn't ask for more."

"Have you seen that outlaw I warned you about? The Campbells who own that ranch across the river say that rustlers got some of their cattle and killed two of their hands, injured three more. They think he did it."

Dessie did not know how to deny that without admitting the outlaw lived on her property, so she said, "I'm sure the sheriff will catch the guilty party and bring him to justice."

"Hanging's too good for a rustler, 'specially a murdering one," the shopkeeper muttered as he finished transferring the eggs. "I've got customers who will be thrilled to know that you've brought in a fresh batch of eggs. Why, Mrs. Gillespie says your hens' eggs taste better than anyone else's. And the Hamptons just dote on the butter you make. What breed of cow did you say you use?"

"Jersey," she replied. "My mother's parents brought

over a bull and four heifers when they emigrated from England to establish a herd here."

"Well, they're somethin' else, Miss Humphrey. You must have quite the tidy operation going on your farm."

"It's small," she said, getting an uneasy feeling between her shoulders. The shopkeeper had never pried into her affairs before and she wondered why he would start now.

"It's an awful lot of work for a woman alone, even with a farmhand. You need a husband to help you out, manage things. I'm a good business man and you're a mighty fine woman, Miss Humphrey."

Ah hah! Someone's looking to own my farm.

"What I have suits me just fine," she replied as she wandered to the rack where ready-made dresses hung near a table hidden beneath an assortment of ladies undergarments. She picked one up.

"That's the latest French design of corset," Mr. Rogers explained. "The ladies say it's more comfortable to wear and gives them that tiny waistline that's so fashionable back east."

Dessie set the garment back down, unable to imagine squeezing her innards like that. She didn't see how anything so constricting could be remotely comfortable. Perusing the dozen dresses hanging on the rack, she realized that each of them was sewn for a corseted figure. With a sigh, she meandered over to the bolts of fabric, knowing she'd have to use her old dresses as patterns if she wanted to avoid wearing a corset.

Another customer entered the store as the proprietor lumbered over to her and put his meaty hand on a bolt of fine red fabric. "Now this red wool, Miss Humphrey, would look a treat on you. You're a pretty woman made for bold colors."

"Mr. Rogers, I declare that you promised that bolt of red wool to me," claimed the woman who had just entered with a younger woman about Dessie's age. She glanced at

Dessie and tilted her head to one side, "Are you that Humphrey girl?"

"Good afternoon, ma'am," Dessie said and decided to take the bait. "Yes, ma'am, I'm Dessie Humphrey. And you are?"

The woman drew herself up in the starchy manner of a respected matron. "I'm Mrs. Daniel Schmidt. My husband owns the town's newspaper and the sawmill. I heard your father passed away. Please accept my condolences."

"Thank you, ma'am."

"Can we expect you to move into town now? A remote farm's no place for a woman alone."

Good manners prevented Dessie from pinching the bridge of her nose in response to the nosy prying. Instead, she affected a small, empty smile and replied, "I have no plans to abandon my family's farm."

"Then you'll be getting married," Mrs. Schmidt said with a nod. "Who's the lucky gentleman?"

"I heard Mr. Ostwich say he intends to marry her," the girl beside Mrs. Schmidt volunteered. "I also heard she's got a man working on the farm and living with her."

"Ostwich!" the shop's proprietor echoed in surprise. "Why that slimy lawyer—"

Dessie gave in to rudeness and interrupted. "I've not agreed to any man's suit."

Really, she thought, that farm was more of a burden than anything else. It hadn't really felt like home since Papa died. However, she hated being bullied.

"A woman ought not live by herself or alone with a man who isn't her husband or immediate family," Mrs. Schmidt cautioned. "Unsavory rumors will ruin a young lady's good reputation."

Dessie shot an angry glance at the matron. "I've done nothing shameful. Are you insinuating otherwise?"

Mrs. Schmidt sniffed in haughty disapproval and her daughter tittered behind her hand.

Mr. Rogers' blustered, "Now, see here, Miss Humphrey's always been a good girl. Why, I'm a respectable man and I've offered to marry her myself!"

Disgusted with the conversation and wanting it to end, Dessie said in a crisp, businesslike tone, "I'll take this bolt of red wool, if you don't mind, Mr. Rogers, and some thread to match. I'll need a bolt of white muslin, too. And I'm not marrying anybody to save my reputation from something I haven't done or to cater to any man's greed."

With an offended huff, Mr. Rogers carried the fabric to the counter. Dessie quickly found some other goods she fancied, including a tin of oysters and concluded the transaction. Thanksgiving was coming up and she thought she'd make her mother's oyster stuffing as a special treat for the holiday. For all her faults and silly notions, Mama had been a wonderful cook and taught her daughter everything she knew.

Mr. Rogers helped load her purchases in the wagon, and John met her in front of the house when she returned.

"That's a purty color," he commented when he spied the bolt of red fabric.

"I was always partial to red," she replied with a shy smile and stroked the fabric. It felt *good* to indulge in something she wanted, rather than only needed.

"Nice lady like you ought to have what she likes," John murmured under his breath as he helped carry in her purchases.

They soon settled back into the same routine as before. They finished planting the winter wheat. Thanksgiving came and went. Cold winds began to howl and snow fell, turning a harsh landscape into one of stark, chiaroscuro beauty. John whittled his fanciful figurines by the firelight and pondered what he'd give his pretty employer for Christmas while she bent her head over a pile of fabric, whether it consisted of mending or sewing.

He watched her as often as he could without being

obvious about doing so, fascinated by the play of firelight upon her gentle features, the soft gloss of her honey-colored hair, and the way her slender figure filled out her dress. The ease with which she moved informed him as nothing else could that she did not wear a corset. He found he rather liked the gentle curve of her figure compared to the exaggeration imposed by a tightly laced corset.

Dessie found herself admiring her employee, a man with rough manners, but who treated her gently, kindly, and with simple courtesy. He *listened* to her when she spoke, without dismissing her words as the frivolous nonsense of a silly girl with naught but fluff between her ears. He actually conversed with her, accorded her opinions equal weight to his. His genuine respect for her warmed her heart. She caught herself admiring the hawk's beak of a nose, the hard amber of his eyes, the breadth of his chest and shoulders, the trim waist, and long legs.

Aside from the full, bushy tangle of his beard, John McClintock was a fine figure of a man.

Neither dared let the other know of their mutual attraction.

The second week of December, he went into town to indulge in a little shopping and visited the bathhouse. A look in the mirror made him grimace. He called over one of the attendants and requested a shave after he soaked and scrubbed himself from top to toe. He donned the new shirt and pants he'd recently acquired and rubbed his clean shaven jaw. He ignored the sounds coming from the other side of the privacy screen.

"Well, well, well," purred one of the whores who served the bathhouse. "Ain't you a purty-faced man?"

John nodded in thanks for the compliment as he gathered his belongings.

"You got some coin on ya, I'll be happy to give yer a discount upstairs," she offered, licking her lips. Most of her customers didn't present such a fine figure, nor were they often freshly bathed.

"I appreciate the offer, ma'am, but I've got to get back home."

John smiled at the word: *home*. It felt good, damned good, especially knowing who waited for him there.

The whore pouted in disappointment.

He pulled on his coat and jammed his hat on his head and headed outside. His spurs jingled as he headed toward the livery where he'd stabled his horse. After paying the hostler for the short loan of a stall and some oats for the horse, John headed back home. There was that word again: *home*. He grinned like a fool. As he neared the homestead, he heard a gunshot. The hairs on the back of his neck prickled. Dessie couldn't shoot the broad side of a barn at point blank distance. Something was wrong if she were firing a gun. Someone firing a weapon at Dessie didn't bear thinking about.

He spurred his horse into a gallop, only slowing when he saw the barn door wide open. Fresh hoofprints in the newly fallen snow tracked toward the barn. He dismounted and led his horse around the backside of the barn, listening hard. He heard a muffled scream and some shouting. The other animals in the barn shifted restlessly, snuffling and huffing and grunting in bestial anxiety. Their sounds masked his. Inching forward to the open doors, he eased both revolvers from their holsters and cocked the hammers.

"Hold her still, boys. I don't want to hurt her," a male voice wafted through the open door.

Peering around the edge of the door, John saw two rough looking men holding *his* woman. She growled and hissed as she struggled. With his back turned toward the door, a well-dressed man approached her and took her chin in his hand. Dessie's gun lay on the floor. The man kicked it away.

"William Ostwich, you won't get away with this," Dessie snarled, trying to wrench her face from his grip.

"Now, Dessie, I tried to be nice about this, but you just wouldn't cooperate. Soon as I ruin you, you'll have to marry me, and then I can sell your farm. It'll fetch a tidy sum, more'n enough to pay my debts."

She growled again, an animalistic sound, and struggled against the two men who held her.

"If you cooperate nicely, I won't give you to my associates here."

"Boss, you promised you'd share," one of the men whined in protest.

John had heard enough. Crouching low, he swung into the barn and shot in rapid succession. The finely dressed man went down first, crumpling as the lead bullet penetrated layers of fabric and flesh to pierce his heart. John felt no remorse for shooting the man in the back. Before the other two men could release their struggling captive and reach for their guns, liquid red blossomed on their chests and they collapsed.

Dessie's chest heaved as she dropped to her knees, the bitter smell of cordite filling her nose. She looked up to see the silhouette of a tall, broad-shouldered man in the doorway.

Trembling, she called out, "John?"

Holstering his guns, he rushed forward and wrapped his arms around her. "Dessie? Dessie, are you all right?"

To his utter horror, she did something he'd never seen her do, despite the hardships they faced on the farm. She buried her face in his shoulder and wept. John could do nothing more than hold her close and murmur repeatedly that she was safe now.

"I've got you, sweetheart. I'll always protect you."

Finally, she sniffled and tilted her head back to look him in the face. He raised a hand and wiped the tears with his thumb.

"Do you mean that?" she whispered.

Although her eyes were luminous with tears, he thought she'd never looked so lovely.

"I mean that," he promised. "I won't let anyone hurt you, ever."

She sighed and leaned her cheek against him. Her arms crept up and encircled him. They remained there for a long, long moment in the comforting embrace.

"You shaved your beard," she finally murmured, leaning back to stroke his jaw with light fingertips, barely refraining from gawking at his handsome visage. "I like seeing your face."

"I'm glad," he replied and pressed a kiss to her forehead. He wished he dared kissed her properly, but she'd had a nasty fright.

She blinked, and expressions he couldn't read flitted across her face in swift succession to settle upon one of firm decision.

"John McClintock, if you're going to stay around that long, then you ought to make an honest woman of me."

John blinked in surprise. "Did you just ask me to marry you?"

She smiled with a hint of that sharp humor she so seldom had opportunity to display. "No, as your employer, I'm ordering you to marry me."

He chuckled. "Well, boss, I can't rightly refuse a direct order, now can I?"

She lost her certainty. "Marry me only if you really want to, John."

He hugged her close again. "I want to more than anything, Dessie, more than anything."

"Then you'd best kiss me properly."

He did, and didn't know where he found the strength to do no more than that. When they pulled apart, he glanced at the dead bodies on the barn floor.

"Something will have to be done about them."

"And you're a wanted man," she added. Squaring her

shoulders, she said, "Leave it to me. I'll take care of this."

It went against his grain to let a woman take care of his problem, but John knew better than to succumb to stupid pride.

"I'll help you."

She nodded. After taking care of John's horse, they loaded the bodies into the wagon and drove the grisly load to the sheriff's office in town. The sheriff twisted the ends of his luxuriant mustache as Dessie explained what happened. He examined the bodies in the back of the wagon and identified them as the two rustlers who'd been plaguing the area and had murdered several wranglers trying to protect their herds.

"Just about everyone knows you're a bad shot, Miss Dessie," the man said and looked at the man standing beside the wagon, a woolen scarf concealing his face. "So, who shot them?"

"My employee," she replied. "He saved me."

"And his name is?" the sheriff prompted. "And how long you been living with a man, Miss Dessie?"

"John McClintock," the gunslinger said, stepping forward, eyes hard and jaw clenched. Dessie reached out and took his hand in hers. "And I've lived on the farm since July."

"Lotta men by that name, I reckon," the sheriff drawled and looked at Dessie, who apparently trusted the man. He'd known her father as smart and sensible and the young woman to be the same, so Dessie's trust counted for a lot in his opinion. He nodded toward the wanted poster that could be seen through the glass panes.

"Large clan," John replied.

"Thought so." The sheriff leveled a sober glare at the younger man. "You take good care of Miss Dessie here, and you'll get no trouble from me."

John nodded. "I intend to take very good care of her. I protect what's mine."

The sheriff nodded, having come to an understanding

with the outlaw. "See that you do." He glanced back at the wagon's contents. "Looks like we'll be needin' a new lawyer. Never did like that one anyway. Smarmy."

He turned his focus to Dessie. "You get that man to the church to speak them vows, you hear? Soon's I get the deputy to take custody of them bodies, I'll collect the missus and we'll witness your marriage."

The sheriff bullied the preacher into an impromptu wedding ceremony witnessed by himself and his wife. John and Dessie returned to the farm to perform the necessary evening chores of caring for the livestock. After supper, he helped her tidy the kitchen and wash the dishes. Then, with a gentle touch, he led her to the bed her parents had once occupied, twice as big as the narrow bed she'd always used.

"I'm nervous," she admitted.

"I know," he replied and stroked her cheek.

"I've never done this before."

"I know."

"I've heard it hurts."

He gathered her to him in a gentle hug and replied, his lips brushing her hair, "I'll distract you."

With a light touch of his fingertips under her jaw, he lifted her face. Bending down, he kissed her and let heat and desire build until she melted against him. Slowly, gently, he undressed her and removed his own clothes. He lowered her to the bed and distracted her until she noticed nothing but sublime pleasure.

John confessed to himself that he'd experienced only pleasure, too. When they came together again in the early light of dawn, he knew he'd found *home*. And so had Desdemona Ophelia Antoinette Humphrey McClintock.

Pride and Peace

It's an open secret on the Lazy Five that Jessie North is a woman, but that doesn't stop Daniel Harper from reacting badly when he learns about it. Can he overcome his prejudice when the proud half-breed saves his life?

"Cordell, you got a minute?" Daniel Harper asked his foreman. Being the newest hire on the Lazy Five, he didn't want to stir up trouble.

The foreman, a man around Daniel's age who had his eye on the boss' daughter, got to his feet and replied, "Sure, Dan."

Dan followed the man who still carried a tin cup full of coffee. They walked to the picket line, a good distance from the campfire, for privacy.

"What is it?" Cordell asked without preamble.

"It's … well, it's about Jesse."

Cordell raised a blond eyebrow. "Yeah?"

"Well, I was washin' up in the creek and … well … I saw *her*." Dan looked around to assure himself that no one listened in. "Jesse's *female*."

"Yeah, we know," came the laconic reply.

"But ... but—"

"But nothin', Dan. The whole crew knows. She's like a little sister to all of us, and iff'n you think to bother her, don't."

"But she's a girl!" Dan protested, every particle of his being outraged and offended. He'd thought himself going loco because something about the *boy* attracted him.

"Yeah, we know." The foreman took a sip of his now-tepid coffee. He sighed, because he went through this with every new hire, especially the handsome, cocky ones like Daniel who enjoyed a little too much popularity with the ladies in town. "She does her job and does it well. So, what's the problem?"

Daniel frowned, because he couldn't very well complain about the girl not doing the job she got paid for. Cordell Johansen was right: she did it and did it as well as or better than anyone else on the crew.

"Does Mr. Bodeen know?"

Cordell eyes narrowed at the implied threat. "If you're thinking of snitching to the boss, then let me reassure you that he'll weigh the value of a good employee who's worked for him for the last three years over a new hire lookin' to make trouble."

Dan clenched his jaw at the not so subtle threat against his continued employment if he didn't keep the communal secret.

"It ain't right," he said finally.

"Look, Dan, you've been a good wrangler in the five months since I hired you. You're a good worker and honest. You know cattle and take good care of your horse. You're smart, too. All them qualities make you a valuable member of the Lazy Five crew and a contender for foreman when I move on. If you get over yerself for a moment, you'll realize that Jessie's good, too—and she's got an advantage that most of us ain't."

Interest piqued, Dan asked, "Oh, what?"

"I ain't never seen a better shot than that woman. She's fast and accurate."

Dan blinked.

"Let me tell you a story, a true story," the foreman said. "Three years ago, we were driving cattle up the Chisolm Trail. Some farmers and merchants who objected to our longhorns passin' through Missouri attacked. Anyway, we were outnumbered and bullets were flyin' hot and fast. I didn't know Jessie was a girl then; I thought she was just a boy who hadn't grown into his beard yet, an orphan, mebbe, who had nothing but his daddy's guns and his daddy's horse. But she reacted to the attack like nothin' I ever saw before. Damn near every bullet she let fly killed someone who was tryin' to keep us from doing our job. She saved our hides that night."

Cordell took a sip of his now-tepid coffee, frowned, and dumped the remainder of the cool, bitter liquid on the ground. He looked at his newest hire who returned his regard with a look of extreme skepticism.

"So, how'd you find out Jessie was female?"

"She was wounded that night. I tended her."

"So, she owes you her life."

The foreman gestured with his empty hand toward the wranglers gathered around the campfire. "Prolly we'd all be dead if it weren't for Jessie North. Her pa was Luther North and her uncle was Capt. Frank North."

"So?" Dan scratched his head at the unfamiliar name.

"Even Wild Bill Hickock couldn't match Frank. That girl's got gun smoke running through her veins." Since the look of disbelief hadn't faded from the new man's expression, Cordell elaborated. "Capt. North and Luther led a troop of Pawnee scouts. It weren't regulation, but Luther's daughter tagged along with them. She been raised among Indian warriors and U.S. soldiers, and they taught her ever'thing they knew."

Dan scratched his head again, trying to absorb the oddity of a woman who understood soldiering and gunfighting and resenting that no one had let him in on the secret sooner. "If you say so."

Cordell leveled a cold look at the other man. "You got any reason to complain about the job she's doin'?"

The wrangler shook his head. He wracked his brain for some valid complaint regarding the woman's performance, but he came up with nothing. The foreman nodded.

"You just continue to think of Jessie as one of the boys and you'll be fine. If anyone in the crew catches you harrassin' her, then we'll miss a good wrangler."

Dan's blood turned cold. "Is that a threat?"

"Let's just say that the last hand who thought Jessie was fair game never finished the cattle drive."

"Who killed him?"

"Who d'ya think?"

Cordell clapped the man on the shoulder and walked back to the campfire, summarily ending the conversation. With a few concise whispers, he advised the hands to keep an eye out.

"What's up, Cordell?" Jessie asked when he took a seat next to her in front of the crackling flames after pouring himself another cup of coffee. She raised her tin cup and took a sip. At his small sigh, her eyes narrowed. "The new wrangler don't like workin' with a female?"

He turned his pale blue eyes toward her. Nighttime shadows poorly illuminated by the flickering of firelight did not reveal her expression, but he dared settle a hand on her shoulder with all the familiarity of a brother. He felt her tension.

"No, he don't," he confirmed, refusing to lie to her.

She nodded, a single jerk of her head. "He got complaints about how I do my job?"

"No, Jessie. You know it ain't that."

She sighed. Not for the first time, she wanted to curse

her father and uncle for her unconventional—*scandalous*—upbringing and education. But her father couldn't leave his half-breed bastard daughter with his wife to raise. She supposed again, and not for the first time, that she ought to have been grateful he took responsibility for her. She sighed again. She grew tired of having to prove every single day that she wasn't just some useless squaw.

As though discerning the direction of her thoughts, the foreman whispered, "We'll watch out for you."

"Thanks, Cordell," she replied, knowing the only true protection she'd get was from her own wits and bullets.

He watched her as she finished her coffee and rinsed the cup in the bucket Walt, the chuckwagon cook, filled each night just for that purpose. She hung the mug by its handle on a peg in an open box on the chuckwagon's side, then headed off to catch some sleep before her shift at watching the herd.

It would take a strong man to take that woman to wife, Cordell thought. He rubbed his nose as he thought of Louisa, the boss' daughter who was everything a young lady ought to be: soft, pretty, and content to keep house for man and raise his children. It didn't hurt that she came with a dowry sufficient to buy his own spread.

A light tap against the sole of her boot woke Jessie. Rolling from her bedroll, she nodded at the wrangler whose shift she would take over and took a moment to adjust her clothing and her gun belt. The heavy weapons pulled at her hips, but the familiar weight reassured her of her equality to the hard men with whom she worked. Father always said that a man's strength didn't matter to a bullet, she just needed to be fast and accurate.

And she was. She'd practiced every day since she was a little girl—and her guns were *always* close at hand.

She inhaled a lungful of moist night air redolent with the sour stench of cattle. Carrying her saddle and bridle to the picket line, she found her horse. Speaking softly, she quieted the animal while she settled the heavy saddle on its back. It endured the quick tug of the girth being cinched without protest. Jessie slid the halter off, put the bridle on, and then slid the halter back over the bridle. With the ease of daily practice, she swung into the saddle and slid her booted feet into the stirrups.

"Come daylight, I'll pick your hooves," she promised the horse.

A few minutes later she touched the brim of her hat to let the wrangler know she was ready to take over. He returned the gesture and set his mount to a slow jog toward the picket line to take care of his horse before he settled down for what was left of the night.

She patrolled the perimeter of the vast herd, setting her mount after those ornery cows that wandered off to round them up and drive them back. It was slow, quiet work interrupted with moments of explosive action. She idly wondered if God had made a less intelligent animal than a cow, then decided that He had: chickens. If ever a species of domesticated livestock deserved to die, it was chickens.

If only they didn't taste so good.

She chuckled softly to herself as her hips swayed with the horse's movement. The hours passed and weariness dragged at Jessie's attention and drained her energy. She'd be glad when they finally delivered the cattle to the stock-yards in Kansas City.

A dark flicker of shadowy movement in her peripheral vision caught her eye. Without speaking, she reined her horse to a halt and listened as her uncle's soldiers had taught her. Below the natural sounds of the herd, the loud chirp of crickets, the unending hum of cicadas, and the soughing of the wind over the prairie, she heard the hushed murmur of masculine voices where none of the Lazy Five crew patrolled. Jessie looked back toward the campsite. *Too far.* Two thousand head of cattle occupied a lot of space.

Jessie looked around again and saw another rider. Squinting to piece out the details to identify him as friend or foe, she thought she recognized him as the new wrangler, the one who'd complained about her just hours ago. Pursing her lips as she pondered the wisdom of enlisting his assistance, she wasted vital seconds making a decision.

Cuing her horse to a working trot, she approached the wrangler and eased her mount alongside his. He looked at her, moonlit expression not welcoming in the least.

"What do you want, Jessie?" he asked, his voice flat and resentful.

Without wasting any additional time to soothe his feelings, she whispered, "We got company. Head back to camp and notify Cordell."

"I ain't doin' what you say, *girl.*"

She shrugged. "Then cover me."

Jessie angled her horse toward a cluster of bushes and slid from the saddle. She dropped her reins, confident the well-trained animal wouldn't wander far. Then she crouched and went very still.

Dan watched the woman and wondered what she was doing. He blinked against the tricky illumination of moonlight as she went still and, a second later, seemed to disappear as though she melted into the shadows and became one with the darkness. He shook his head and peered more intensely where her horse stood. But he saw nothing.

"Well, shit," he muttered under his breath. "She's probably turned an ankle and needs to be rescued. Foolish woman."

He directed his horse toward her and pulled alongside the beast. When he looked at the ground, Jessie was nowhere near. Her rifle remained in its saddle-mounted holster.

"Well, shit," he said again and peered over the tall grass

and dark lumps that indicated individual cows. A smudge of shadow caught his eye. *That wasn't a cow.*

Daniel headed toward it, setting the horse to a brisk walk. As he moved forward, she zigzagged toward a dip in the rolling landscape, a barely discernible flow of shadow. The stealthy way she moved convinced him that the Pawnee had indeed taught her something of their sneaky warfare tactics.

After a few minutes of spotty tracking of her progress, he heard her voice, clear and cold, float on the late summer breeze: "Drop your weapons."

A split second later, the *crack* of a pistol woke every beast and man within a square mile. A scream split the air, followed by shouts and profane curses. Three more shots followed in quick succession as Dan spurred his horse into a gallop toward the ruckus.

Hearing the thunder of hard-pounding hooves, she turned toward Dan as he hauled back on the reins to stop the beast.

"There's two more," she barked at him, her voice icy and clipped.

He looked at the four recumbent lumps of shadow lying still on the ground, the moonlight giving pale evidence of a cold camp. "How do you know?"

"There's sign of six horses," she replied and jammed her guns back into their holsters. "Now *git*!"

He wheeled his horse around just as a ululating cry broke out, startling the cattle. As one massive, alarmed entity, the herd surged to its feet. He heard the pounding of Jessie's boots as she ran toward her horse. The cattle milled about, frightened and confused. A gunshot from the far side of the herd reverberated, accompanied by a shouting voice. Another shot fired into the air broke the animals' collective nerve and the herd thundered away from the frightening sounds.

"Stampede!" Dan heard someone's high-pitched cry. He

gaped at the direction the heaving bodies and hard hooves took and spurred his horse into another hard gallop after Jessie. He didn't want to see anyone trampled to death, not even a woman who didn't know her proper place.

Panicked by the stampede, Jessie's horse bolted. Lungs burning as she ran for the bushes in desperate hope that the cattle wouldn't trample those—and her with them— Jessie did not distinguish the sound of equine hooves from bovine until a hard arm slammed into her and hauled her off the ground.

"Hang on!" Dan shouted as she slammed into the saddle and across his thighs. His horse grunted and stumbled at the sudden addition of extra weight. The galloping horse squealed as a sharp horn gouged its flank. The cries of wranglers trying to corral the massive herd pierced the air above the roar of pounding hooves. They heard more gunfire and a horse screamed. Jessie hoped it wasn't hers.

She clung to her insecure perch on the new wrangler's lap as she tried to see what was going on. But the heaving bodies of panicked cattle obscured her view and all her other senses. The horse stumbled again, its wounded leg buckling.

"He's going down!" she shouted at Daniel as she wrenched a gun free and fired into the air over the stampeding cattle in an effort to direct them away from the injured horse.

The wrangler's response was to give his mount a vicious jab with his spurs. The beast responded with another squeal and a grunt as it tried to comply with its rider's need. As the cattle swerved to get away from the scary noises spewing from Jessie's gun, another widespread horn crashed into flesh and the leg collapsed, sending the horse and its riders crashing to the ground. Dan shoved his passenger off his lap as the horse crumpled. The horse squealed again and thrashed its legs, unable to rise. Dan felt pain explode in his leg which was trapped beneath the terrified animal.

"I'm trapped!" he shouted.

Jessie grunted as she picked herself off the hard earth. She opened and closed both fists, hating that she'd lost her gun when she hit the ground. She'd lost her hat, too. Every muscle protested as she hobbled to Dan's side. She paused by the struggling horse and knew that it would never stand again. With regret for the loss of a good animal, she drew her remaining pistol and shot it.

"What the hell?" Dan demanded.

"It's leg is broken," she answered and walked around the beast.

"Well, I'm still trapped!"

"I'll find my horse and get you out."

"You can't leave me here!"

"I can't roll that carcass over by myself," she replied and turned away. The click of a hammer being cocked made her freeze. "Shooting me won't help."

"You can't leave me here," he repeated.

She gazed into the distance, but didn't really see anything. Finding her horse wouldn't be easy. Turning around, she approached him again and kneeled next to him.

"I won't leave you."

The relief Dan felt was palpable. "I think my leg is broken."

"It might be," she replied, her voice cool and unconcerned.

"You're a cold bitch, ain't you?" he snapped.

She looked at him, the darkness rendering her expression inscrutable but for the angry gleam of her eyes. "Would weeping and wailing help?"

He sighed and looked away. "No."

"Right then."

She sat on the dead horse's flank and ran her hand over the smooth, sweat-soaked hide as she listened to the thunder of hooves and the shouts of men and the occasional crack of gunfire. *At least the cattle turned away from us and we're alive.*

Daniel wondered at her quiet. *I never spent time with a woman who didn't chatter my ear off.*

"I shoulda known it were a dirty injun that sneaked up on Bart and the others," rasped a voice from behind them. "You killed my brothers and now I'm gonna kill you!"

Jessie reached for her remaining pistol and whirled around, then cried out as blistering pain fired through her upper arm. Eyes narrowed, she fired back.

"Y-you're a woman," the filthy and battered rustler gasped in surprise as he clutched at his chest and toppled over onto Dan who couldn't move out of the way. He grunted and shoved, pain and nausea shooting through his body like nothing else he'd ever felt.

Feeling hot blood run down her arm, Jessie dropped the pistol back into its holster. She hissed as movement aggravated the pain. She rose to her feet and fisted a handful of soiled, damp fabric in the hand of her good arm. Grunting, she dragged the man off Daniel.

"Thank you," he muttered and looked with distaste at the rustler's blood that had soaked through his own shirt. He glanced with burgeoning respect at the woman who'd saved his life. "He would have shot us both."

"He shouldn't have gotten so close. I was distracted. Sorry."

Daniel gaped at the laconic apology. "Uh … your arm."

She glanced at it, the sleeve now fully drenched and sticking unpleasantly to her arm. Flies would soon swarm. She tugged at her neckerchief and kneeled beside him.

"Do you think you can tie it for me?"

He shoved himself into a sitting position, sweating in agony and none too sure that he could remain sitting upright. "I'll try."

"Looks like the bullet went all the way through." His hands trembled as he wrapped the folded cloth snugly around her arm and tied it. She grunted, but otherwise made no protest.

"You're tough," he said in reluctant admiration.

"Yeah," she replied, her voice distant. She'd always had to be tough.

Jessie plundered the accessible saddlebag to retrieve what few of the wrangler's belongings she could. She blinked at the pouch that jingled with coins, but said nothing. She simply piled everything next to Daniel.

That task finished, she turned around in the opposite direction to look out for anyone else who might approach. They remained there in silence as the hours passed and dawn illuminated the eastern horizon.

Having nothing better to do, Daniel watched Jessie. He observed the straight line of her nose, the firm set of her chin, and the pinched lips and pallor brought on by pain, blood loss, and weariness. A bruise darkened the left side of her face. Her dusty black hair escaped from its long braid. Her shoulders and spine remained straight and unbowed. He watched as she scanned the horizon in all directions.

"Are you looking for something specific?"

"Either a horse, one of the crew, or that sixth rustler."

He nodded and swallowed, and wished he could reach his canteen, but it was under the horse next to his leg. They lapsed into silence again. A cow lowed in the distance. Essentially stuck in one position, Daniel contented himself with watching Jessie watch everything else. He thought he'd never seen anyone—man or woman—so self-contained.

"I'll be back," she announced and rose to her feet.

"What? Where are you going?" Daniel felt ashamed of his sudden panic, but he truly did not want to be left alone and vulnerable to anything with two or four legs that might consider him prey.

"I see a horse," the quiet reply floated back to him.

Unable to do more than sit there, he watched as Jessie walked slowly away. He noticed she limped. He hadn't noticed any blood on her trousers, so didn't think she'd been shot. Perhaps hitting the ground at a gallop had simply bruised her. She zigzagged, paused, and picked something up off the ground. She repeated the process and picked up something else. After a moment, he realized that Jessie had retrieved her lost pistol and her hat.

Her absence gave his bladder the reprieve it demanded. Although he burned with shame, he could no longer hold back the release of urine that soaked his pants and the dirt beneath him. At least Jessie was not there to witness his shame.

He soon lost sight of her and worried until he heard the quiet tread of hooves approach. Sitting in the still morning with crickets chirping and cicadas buzzing, he found himself surprised at what he could hear and distinguish from the other noises.

Jessie's scuffed, dusty boots led a sorrel with three white legs towards him. He looked up. Jessie swayed slightly. The horse jigged, restive and upset at being near the carcass of his horse.

"You need to rest," he said.

"Can't." She patted the horse's neck and made her way around the off side of the nervous beast. She untied the lariat from the saddle and, still speaking in soothing tones to the horse, tossed Dan one end.

"Tie that to whichever hoof you can reach," she ordered as she wrapped the other end around the pommel.

He did as she bade him and let her know when the rope was secure. Jessie led the horse around the carcass and then, swinging into the saddle, urged it forward. Skittish, but obedient, the horse did as she asked. When the rope went taut, the horse jigged again. However, Jessie expected the horse to react, and maintained a calm and soothing demeanor to prevent the anxious animal from bolting. Word by word, pat by stroke, the horse moved foot by foot forward, rolling the stiffened carcass over. When the dead horse landed with a thud on its other side and Daniel cried out from a new surge of pain, the horse's haunches launched the beast into a panicked bolt.

Jessie hissed as she held onto the pommel for dear life, the strain tearing at her injured arm. However, she allowed the lariat to release from the saddle horn so the horse no longer needed release from the carcass it dragged. With weary patience, she calmed the animal and brought it back to her hand. Sweating and trembling, the horse eventually listened to her and allowed her to ride it near the man on the ground and the carcass.

"Get what you need from the other saddlebag," she said.

He dragged himself into place and opened the saddle-bag. He pulled out a grubby change of clothes and a few other odds and ends. He glanced at the crushed canteen.

"I need to change," he said.

She nodded and turned her head. He trusted she would respect his privacy as he stripped and changed. He had to slit the seam of his pant leg to slide over the boot on his injured leg. Only the leather shaft of his boot kept the swelling in check. He decided to leave the soiled clothing behind.

"I'm done."

"Can you stand?" she asked him.

Daniel took a deep breath. "I think so."

She sidled the horse closer to him. Weary and defeated, the animal obeyed. She patted its shoulder and leaned back to empty the saddlebags the sorrel carried. She discarded everything except a good quality bowie knife and leather pouch of tobacco and papers. At her glance, Daniel stuffed his possessions into the saddlebag.

"Use my leg and the saddle to steady yourself. You'll have to haul yourself up behind me. I can't lift you."

He nodded and did as she suggested. Breathing hard and sweating profusely, he finally pulled himself over the horse's rump and slid his leg around so that he sat over the animal's loins behind the saddle. Clamping his hands over the cantle, he tried not to think that he touched Jessie's backside through the dirty canvas of her britches. He tried not to think of how he'd groped her leg as he used her to steady himself. He tried to ignore the pungent smell of urine that wafted from his discarded trousers and found himself again grateful that she did not remark upon his disgrace, even though he was certain she had noticed. She seemed to notice everything.

"You all right back there?" she asked, her voice wavering with exhaustion.

"Yeah."

She clucked her tongue and the horse moved forward.

"Where we goin'?" he asked.

"We'll rejoin the crew. Cook keeps some medicines and bandages in the chuckwagon. Maybe they'll have found my horse. I need a wash and a change of clothes and so do you."

He grunted, because she spoke nothing less than the truth.

He did not know how long they rode, but the heat of the day already beat down upon them when they finally caught up with the cattle drive. Once again, he appreciated how she didn't fill the quiet with inane chatter.

"Hey, it's Jessie!" one of the wranglers shouted and wheeled his horse around to gallop toward them. When he caught up with them and turned his horse to walk alongside theirs, he exclaimed, "We thought you was dead!"

Another horse and rider joined them. Cordell.

"Your horse returned without a rider. We thought you were dead."

"Not quite," she mumbled, swaying in the saddle.

His gaze latched onto the bloody sleeve. "I'll take you

to Walt."

She did not protest when he pulled her from the saddle and sat her across his thighs in front of him.

"Daniel's hurt, too," she muttered.

"Okay, Jessie. I'll take care of things," the foreman answered. Relieved of her duty, Jessie released her fading grip on consciousness and slumped in Cordell's arms. He adjusted his hold on her to manage his mount's reins and looked at the injured man. "Daniel, can you follow us?"

Daniel nodded and heaved himself forward into the saddle, grunting when the movement jarred his injured leg. He asked for a drink of water and the foreman handed him his canteen.

"What happened?" Cordell asked as he gulped down the water.

"Jessie caught some rustlers," Daniel replied. He capped the canteen and handed it back.

"I figured that much," Cordell replied in a dry tone. "*Then* what happened?"

"She was on foot. Her horse bolted in the stampede. I got her out of that, but a beef gored my horse. I pushed Jessie out of the way, but the horse fell on my leg. Then she killed one of the rustlers who came to get his revenge. I never saw nothin' like it."

"You gonna complain about working with a woman again?"

Daniel shook his head. "She saved my life."

He looked at her, eyes gleaming with a discomfiting mixture of shame and admiration. "She's amazing. Hell, I'd marry her if she'd ever want me."

The foreman shifted the woman he carried and replied in a low voice, "She's a grand girl, but no man will ever want her as his wife. After a day's hard work, a man wants to come home to something soft and sweet, and Jessie ain't never been soft nor sweet."

Looking at the woman in the foreman's arms, Daniel

saw her expression congeal into something bleak, even though she remained limp. *Mebbe she ain't as unconscious as we think.*

The other wrangler cantered his horse ahead to way-lay the chuckwagon. He clambered into the driver's seat while the cook climbed into the back to set up his mobile sick ward. The wagon stopped just long enough to transfer the injured into the back and tie a dead rustler's commandeered horse to the tailgate, then Cordell rode off to rejoin the herd.

The cook lifted a pair of saddlebags and pulled out a clean shirt. He looked at Daniel and explained, "When Jessie's horse was found without her, Cordell put her belongings in here. We was gonna ship them to her pa when we reached Kansas City."

Daniel nodded.

"Will ya help me remove her clothes? I gotta check to make sure she ain't hurt nowhere else. If she is, she won't admit it."

Daniel nodded and swallowed. He tried not to notice the soft, feminine flesh revealed to him. He winced at the bruising she'd acquired from her tumble from his horse.

"You tell anyone what you saw in here and I'll gut you with a rusty spoon," Walt threatened.

Daniel nodded. "I'll keep her honor."

The cook leveled a considering look at him. "See that you do. We've had a few of your type at the Lazy Five—too handsome for their own good and thinking they was entitled to any woman what caught their eye."

Daniel's face burned with shame.

He assisted the cook in cleaning and bandaging Jessie's wounded arm, gaped at the long knife scar across her ribs, then helped slip a clean shirt over her. He darted a questioning look at the cook who ignored it and said nothing more than, "It ain't my story to tell."

Daniel nodded and wondered who had cut her and

why. He also wanted to pummel that miscreant into the dirt with his bare fists.

"Now, let's take care of you." Walt turned his attention to Daniel's injured leg. "I'll have to cut that boot off. Can't tell if your ankle's broken less'n I do."

"Do it," Daniel agreed through gritted teeth.

Too long later, the cook determined that Daniel's leg wasn't broken, but the ankle was badly sprained. He wrapped it tightly and dosed his patient with laudanum.

"You rest," Walt said. "Iff'n I remember right, there's a place not too far ahead where we can detour you and Jessie to a nearby town. Cordell keeps some extra coins on hand in case of such contingencies. He'll pay for your stay for a few days, 'til you and Jessie can arrange to get back to the Lazy Five."

Daniel nodded and let the laudanum lull him to sleep.

Jessie awoke before he did. She lay still for a long moment, taking the time she needed to regain awareness of her surroundings: the rattles, clanks, and creaks of the wagon; the clop of hooves and the occasional snort of a horse; the bawling and odor of cattle; the ever-present trail dust that clung to everything; and the brawny arms that wrapped around her. She opened her eyes and looked around, realizing that she knew that musky smell. She rolled over to face the scruffy jaw of the too-handsome man who said he'd marry her. No one had ever said *that* before. She eased back from him and realized that her arm was clean and she wore a clean shirt.

Well, it wasn't the first time Walt had cleaned her up.

"Hey there," came the sleepy rumble from deep within Daniel's chest.

She looked at him again and realized that he'd tilted his head to gaze into her eyes. He blinked. She blinked. He smiled, the sleepiness replaced by a knowing glint.

"You saw me," she whispered, cheeks flushing.

"I did. You're beautiful." He paused, frowned. "Who cut

you?"

"Oh." She averted her eyes, feeling uncommonly shy and vulnerable without the heavy weight of her guns at her hips. "It happened a couple of years ago."

"What happened?" he growled.

"It doesn't matter."

"It does to me."

Jessie sighed. "We had a hand who thought I was there to service the crew."

"I'll kill him," Daniel snarled.

The corner of her mouth curled. "No need. I already did."

He nodded, satisfied that she could take care of herself better than most men. "Good."

He sighed.

"What's that for?"

"What?"

"That sigh. Like you're disappointed or something."

"I feel redundant with you."

"What do you mean?"

He sighed again and tucked her head into his chest and held it there. She did not resist, but neither did she relax. He enjoyed the feeling of her pressed against him and wondered for a second whether she truly relaxed with anyone. She always seemed to be on guard, wary.

"A man's supposed to protect his woman, but you don't need my protection."

She frowned. *Who said I was your woman?*

Daniel continued speaking, the words coming slowly as his thoughts unraveled. "You don't seem to need much of anything or anyone."

Cheek pressed against his chest, Jessie responded with a sad smile. *This is nice.* Instead of saying that, she murmured, "No one's hugged me since I was a child."

His arms tightened around her and he smiled as inspiration struck.

"I know what you need. You need someone to hold you, someone to give you affection, someone you can relax with."

She tilted her head back to look at him and didn't bother to deny it. "You think you're the person who can give that?"

"I'd like to be that person, if you'll have me."

"Not two days ago you hated me."

"Not two days ago I hated myself, because I thought I was feelin' things I ought not to for a boy."

"Oh." Jessie really didn't know how to respond to that.

He sighed. "I was mad and I took it out on you because I thought you deceived me on purpose."

"I did."

Daniel chuckled. "Yeah, you did."

"So, you think you like me?"

"I know I admire you, and I think I could love you," he admitted. "Question is, do you think you could love me back?"

Jessie sighed and pressed her forehead against his chest again. Always honest with herself, she silently admitted that she knew he'd seen her bathing in the creek and she'd *liked* it. She supposed she'd wanted him to know she was a woman, to react to her as a man who admired a woman reacted. She recalled that she liked him before he discovered she was Jessie instead of Jesse. They'd gotten along really well and she enjoyed his dry sense of humor. He was a good worker, honest. He took good care of his horse, putting its welfare before his own. He got along with all the other hands, friendly without being obsequious.

"I don't know."

Daniel winced at her blunt candor. "Would you be willin' to try?"

She tilted her head back and met his eye with her own steady gaze. "Can you accept me as I am? I ain't soft and pretty."

You're strong and beautiful. "If every one of our sons took after you, I'd be the proudest daddy on the continent."

"And our daughters?"

"I hope you'll teach 'em to be strong and resourceful like you."

Her ears and heart detected no dishonesty in his words. She smiled at him. "Daniel Harper, are you askin' me to marry you?"

"If you want someone who'll give you the affection and peace you want, then yes. If you want some excitement, I'll be happy to give you that, too." He waggled his eyebrows suggestively. She giggled, a sound that surprised both of them. "And if you want someone to make you laugh, I'd be honored."

Jessie sighed. "I want all those things."

His arms tightened around her. "Good. And maybe you'll protect me. It's scary out there."

She chuckled and he smiled.

From the driver's seat of the chuckwagon, Walt looked back at the embracing couple and grinned.

"Looks like we'll be planning a weddin' soon," he said under his breath. He hoped the next town had a preacher.

Resurrection

Undertakers bury the dead; they don't resurrect bodies left for dead. But that's exactly what Antonio DiCarlo does when a lovely Swedish immigrant lands on his doorstep.

"Got a delivery for ya, Tony," Cletus Campbell announced as he walked into Antonio diCarlo's office. "Settlers from that immigrant camp near Plum Creek."

Tony accompanied Cletus outside and peered into the older man's wagon. Three bodies lay uncovered, open to the crisp autumn air. Blood crusted their worn clothing. Slack flesh indicated the passage of rigor mortis.

"When?" Tony asked.

"Sometime yesterday morning," came the laconic answer. "Rumor is the Jenkins gang got 'em. Stole their horses and cattle. Shot or destroyed everything else they didn't want or couldn't take with them."

Tony sighed. "Make sure the sheriff knows."

"Sheriff and most folks hereabouts don't care 'bout them immigrants. They'd be just as happy to see 'em gone."

Being an immigrant himself, Tony squelched the flare of temper that Cletus' words ignited. Instead, he pointed out, "The Jenkins gang goes after the settlers camp because it's easy. When they no longer have such easy pickings, they'll come after the families living at the outer edges of town."

Cletus scratched his oily scalp, found a louse, and squeezed its body between filthy fingernails. The man subscribed to neither cleanliness nor godliness. But he was reliable and willing to do the hard, dirty jobs declined by more respectable people.

"Fetch Billy and carry the man out back," Tony said, looking at the pallor of the bodies in the wagon. Something about one of them struck him as inconsistent. "Then you come and get the older woman. I'll carry the girl."

Cletus shrugged and lurched toward the back of the property where Billy pounded nails into a coffin. Tony climbed into the wagon and pressed his fingertips to the young woman's throat ... and waited.

"*Dio in paradiso*," he whispered as his sensitive fingertips detected a faint, thready beat. "*È viva.*"

He hefted the young woman into his arms and clambered down from the wagon as Cletus and Billy walked toward the vehicle.

"After you carry those two to the back, bring the physician here," he ordered.

"Tony, the doc can't bring back the dead," Billy said.

"This one," he nodded to the young woman in his arms, "is not dead. Not yet." He directed a hard glare at the two men. "Say *nothing* of this to anyone but the physician. Tell him it's an emergency."

The two men nodded, knowing that if they didn't do exactly as ordered, they'd not get their daily bottle of whiskey.

Tony carried the girl inside and took her upstairs where he lay her on his own bed. Hurrying, he fetched a pail of water and one of his own washcloths and a cake of soap. Cleanliness was necessary for an undertaker, because the dead often carried disease.

With a lamentable absence of his usual clinical detachment, Tony stripped the body of its bloodstained clothes and tossed them in a corner. He examined her body as he washed it, making note of every bruise, every scrape, every scar. He breathed a sigh of relief when he saw no sign of intimate violation. *Probably they shot her and assumed she was dead. Even hardened criminals prefer to rape living women.* He grimaced at the puckered, swollen flesh around the gunshot wounds and the pallor of a human body that had lost too much blood. He cleaned the soft, pretty, feminine body with care, then covered her with a blanket when he heard the heavy tread of boots on the wooden staircase.

"Cletus says you got one that ain't quite dead," boomed the town's only physician.

Antonio nodded. "She's a survivor of an attack by the Jenkins gang. If they know she lives and can identify them, then they'll hunt her down and anyone else to whom she might speak."

The doctor lay a finger alongside his nose and nodded with a wisdom Tony doubted he truly possessed. "I see. Well, what do you want me to do for her? Finish her off?"

"*Mio Dio, no,*" Tony hissed. "I want you to save her if you can."

"Billy says she's one o' them Swedes from the camp."

"What does that have to do with anything?"

"Might be best for everyone if she don't live. Lotta folks in these parts don't want 'em here."

Millennia of imperial Roman fury shot through Tony's narrowed eyes. The physician took a step back from the undertaker's glare. "Then go. And tell no one about her. If I hear so much as a whisper, I'll let the townsfolk know that you prefer to kill your patients rather than heal them."

Since every family in town dealt with the undertaker

eventually, the doctor understood the ramifications of Tony's threat. Townsfolk liked to brag that they had a trained undertaker from Rome who was versed in the most modern, elegant, *European* ways of sending the dearly departed to their final rest. They ignored his weekly attendance at Catholic Mass with the Mexicans as an odd quirk.

Knowing that neither of the Protestant preachers in town would deign to pray over the girl's dead parents without financial compensation, Tony sent Billy to speak to Father Ramón. The man exemplified the best of a humble priest, reminding Tony of Father Giorgio back in the neighborhood of his childhood.

He whispered thanks to God as he dug bullets from the girl's flesh. She groaned, a weak, pitiful sound, but did not wake. He poured a small measure of grain alcohol over the livid wounds and hoped infection would not set in. He bandaged her, then rolled her over one way and the other to settle her under the covers. For a few seconds, he simply sat beside her on the bed and stroked the lank hair that, once washed, he knew would glow red like the most beautiful sunset he'd ever seen when crossing the ocean from one continent to the other.

He wondered what her name was.

Having made her as comfortable as he could, Tony whispered, "*Arrivederci.*" Then he headed downstairs to give the young woman's parents the best funeral he could manage.

At his bidding, Billy importuned the Spanish priest who greeted Tony with a gentle smile and prayed with strong, simple faith over the immigrants' bodies. He anointed them with holy oil and helped Tony lay them in coffins. He stood by while Tony harnessed and hitched his big, black horse to the funeral wagon for transport to the pauper's cemetery. Cletus and Billy, sent on ahead, finished digging the graves. Tony always kept two or three ready in the pauper's field, because such customers landed on his doorstep with dismal regularity.

Disease, starvation, injury, and hardship claimed many lives. He'd once believed in the ideals of this new country, but that belief had long since lost its luster. Yet, he remembered the entrenched discrimination of his homeland and knew it as being no better. Bella's heavy hooves clopped on the hard-packed dirt road and the black lacquered wagon rattled down the road as he thought about how people were the same the world over.

As always, people watched the elegant equipage roll by. As always, Tony ignored their stares and curiosity.

In shared solemnity, the four men unloaded the two caskets and lowered them into the ground. They doffed their hats and bowed their heads as Father Ramón prayed for their souls. Tony and the priest left Billy and Cletus to fill in the graves as they rode back to the funeral home.

"Father, I have a confession to make," Tony said in a low tone to the black-robed man who sat next to him.

The priest kissed his stole, crossed himself, and replied, "Speak, my son."

Tony spoke, telling him how one of the three bodies brought to him still lived.

"This is a miracle!"

Tony nodded. He thought so, too. He confessed how he had undressed the young woman and let his gaze linger on her flesh.

"It was sinful."

"You are a man," the priest said. "No doubt, you wish to marry and have a family?"

"*Sì.*"

The priest smiled at the foreign word that was the same in both their native languages. He suggested in a gentle tone, "Then perhaps you should see if God has placed this woman into your care for a reason."

"She is Swedish."

"Ah, and therefore a Lutheran."

"*Sì.*"

Father Ramón shrugged. "I would have liked to see you wed one of the lovely *señoritas* in my parish, but perhaps God wills you to love otherwise. Perhaps she will convert and you will save her soul as well as her life?"

Tony bowed his head and accepted the priest's wisdom. One could neither know the will of God nor argue against it.

He dropped the priest off at the edge of town and continued home. The big, black draft horse submitted with her usual ponderous grace to his attention before plodding into her paddock for a good roll. Tony sighed, watching her for a moment, then he headed inside. He heard the melodic humming of the woman who kept house and cooked for him.

"Consuela," he called.

"*Sì?* You had a funeral already today?" she inquired as she emerged from the kitchen wiping her hands on her apron.

He smiled at her, for she reminded him of his favorite aunt. He explained, "Settlers from the immigrant camp."

She frowned, then gave him a small smile. "You are kind to give them a good funeral, *Señor* Antonio."

"One of them survived," he confessed yet again. "A girl. She is badly wounded. I put her in my room. Would you see if you can find some clothing for her ... and other things a young woman needs?"

The older woman patted his arm. "You are a kind man, a good man. Has she eaten?"

He shook his head. "She was not awake when I left."

"Ah. I will fix some broth. You will take that and some bread to her. I will also make you a good stew. You must stay strong to take care of this *señorita.*"

He kissed Consuela on the cheek. "You are magnificent! If I were twenty years older, I would marry you."

"If you were twenty years older, I would let you."

Chuckling, Tony went into his office and retrieved some cash from the locked drawer in his desk. He handed her the money to purchase what his guest needed. With another maternal pat on his arm, she left.

He headed upstairs to check on the woman. She slept. He went back downstairs to his office to finish the paperwork abandoned when Cletus arrived on his doorstep that morning. When he finished with that, he checked on her again. No change. He headed outside to work on building coffins. When he had the time, he created beauty. The wealthy residents in town favored the polished, elegantly carved wood for their dearly departed and were prepared to pay handsomely for the luxurious accommodations. He snorted at his gallows humor when contemplating—not with any seriousness—learning to carve stone so he could fashion elaborate sarcophagi. The obscenely wealthy cattle barons would certainly indulge their vanity by purchasing such extravagances as monuments to their own legends.

He checked on his patient again and ate lunch sitting at her bedside. Perhaps she had rested sufficiently, or perhaps she sensed the presence of another person, or perhaps the aroma of his lunch disturbed her, but her eyelids fluttered open. She blinked and moaned at the pain that pounded with every heartbeat.

"*Var är jag?*" she muttered. "*Är jag död?*"

Tony set down his plate and gaped at the prettiest green eyes he'd ever seen. Although he did not understand a word she said, he assumed she was confused as well as in pain, and probably thirsty.

He held a cup of water to her lips and said, "Drink."

He slid his hand behind her head to help her drink. She took a sip, then another. Water dribbled from her lips and trickled over smooth, pale skin. He gently lowered her head back to the pillow. She blinked again.

"*Vem är du?*"

Guessing as to her questions, he pointed to himself

and said, "Antonio." He pointed at her and said nothing, but gave her a small smile of encouragement. He pressed his fingertip to his chest and repeated his name, then pointed at her. Awareness flickered in her eyes. He pointed to himself and she said, "Antonio." Tony thought her accent charming. He pointed to her and she said, "Linnea." He repeated it, savoring the syllables on his tongue and giving them a Latin inflection she thought charming.

"*Ja.*"

"*Sì.*"

"Är du spansk?"

Tony shook his head, not understanding the question. He held up the cup and offered it to her. She nodded and he helped her drink.

Consuela returned with her arms filled. She smiled when Tony told her that his guest had awakened and spoken with him. She chuckled with him when he informed her that they hardly understood each other. She agreed to look after the girl, because it just wasn't seemly for a bachelor to do so. The undertaker had a respectable reputation to maintain.

Tony returned his attention to business. He sold two of his premade, elegant caskets to the two most prominent families in the area. He took his dinner on a tray at his guest's bedside and enjoyed a slow exchange of words to communicate before thinking to ask her if she spoke English.

"*Ja*, a little," she replied.

He smiled. "Oh, good."

Her expression took on the desperation of hope. "My *mamma*? *Pappa*?"

Understanding that question, Tony shook his head. "Dead."

She closed her eyes and looked away from him. Tears trickled.

"I am sorry," Tony said.

Thankful as she was to have landed in the care of a generous and kind man, Linnea wondered, *What will happen to me?*

Two weeks later and wearing one of Tony's two nightshirts, Linnea went downstairs for the first time. Her ankles and knees wobbled and every muscle trembled. The short journey exhausted her. Consuela, however, greeted her with cheerful smiles and maternal admonitions in rapid Spanish not to overtire herself as she helped Linnea into the kitchen. Assured of privacy—Tony was at a funeral—the undertaker's housekeeper filled buckets with water and helped Linnea bathe. The younger woman relished the feeling of being clean once again, although she frowned at the cake of harsh soap the woman gave her to use.

That evening, she wore a borrowed dress, the simple garb of a Mexican peasant girl, and joined Antonio at the table for supper. Antonio could not take his eyes off her pale beauty and the vibrant fire of her hair hanging loose over her shoulders and down her back. In the same halting manner in which they began, they conversed in an odd mixture of English, Italian, and Swedish.

Determined that she not be a burden on her benefactor, who had slept on a cot in his office every night since her arrival, Linnea assisted Consuela in keeping house, cooking, and washing laundry. She began to add Spanish to her repertoire of languages. Between the two women's efforts, the funeral parlor and Antonio's living quarters were never so clean and tidy, the laundry never so fresh, and the meals never so varied. Antonio found he rather liked the Swedish influence in the foods they served him. The things Linnea could do with cream reminded him of the rare treat of cannoli from his childhood.

Winter descended in icy fury. Cletus and Billy spent long hours chipping at frozen earth to dig graves for those citizens who died and whose families refused to wait for an extended thaw in the weather to bury them. Paupers' frozen bodies were stacked like cordwood to be buried in a mass grave in the spring.

At Antonio's warning, Linnea made sure never to allow anyone but Cletus, Billy, and Consuela see her. Consuela bought fabric that Linnea sewed into two more simple dresses and leather that she fashioned into crude shoes and skeins of yarn that she knitted into hats, mittens, and scarves.

"In the spring I must leave," she announced at dinner.

Tony's fork stopped its ascent, hovering between plate and mouth. He looked at her in astonishment. "Why?"

"It is not appropriate for me to live here. I must work, earn money."

Tony lowered his fork. It clinked when it landed on the plate. He took a deep breath and realized that she was right. She could not remain hidden forever like a dirty secret, and the townsfolk would certainly disapprove. They would not believe both he and she remained chaste. He opened his mouth to suggest marriage, but the glint of pride in her eyes warned him that his suit would not be welcomed, at least not yet.

"You are determined?"

She nodded.

"What will you do? There's not a lot of respectable occupations for women here."

She smiled and pressed her fingertips to her sternum. "I am a skilled soap maker for ladies and gentlemen who prefer fine soaps."

"Soap?" Antonio blinked.

She nodded. "If you will loan me the funds to buy some supplies, I will pay you back."

Antonio shook his head and sighed. "Most households around here make their own soap."

"Not *my* soap." Her voice resonated with pride. "*Ja.* Allow me to purchase some supplies and I will show you."

He wracked his brain and decided that he could spare a corner of his workshop for her enterprise, as long as the cost was not too dear. He made a good living as the town's only undertaker, but he was far from wealthy. He relented and asked, "What do you need?"

The next day, Consuela went shopping. Following Linnea's orders, Billy acquired a barrel. He drilled a narrow hole in one end and set it on two blocks of wood with a bucket beneath the hole. Linnea filled the barrel with several inches of pebbles and then layered several inches of straw over that followed by bucketsful of white ashes from hardwood fires collected from the hearths of Consuela's many relatives. Linnea filled a bucket with water and slowly poured it over the ashes, refilling and pouring until the ash was soaked.

Over the next several hours, water filtered through the ash, straw, and stones to drip into the bucket. When the bucket was nearly full, Linnea swapped it out for an empty bucket. She dipped a feather into the lye water. It dissolved, proving that the lye was strong enough to use.

Meanwhile, in another pot over a fire, fat from beef, chicken, pork, and wild game sizzled and rendered. She strained the liquefied fat through cheesecloth and poured it into a cauldron over a fire. Looking at Consuela, she said, "It is better to use oil from olives or other plants than tallow."

She poured the lye water into the cauldron, taking care not to splash the corrosive liquid. Then she let it simmer for two days. As the liquid boiled, she worked on extracting the fragrant oils from an extravagant purchase of precious oranges and cinnamon sticks. She tossed in salt, which caused the soap to rise and separate from any remaining impurities. Salt would also harden the soap. When she judged the mixture ready, she decanted the paste and boiled it in fresh water with the fragrant oils to refine it even more. When the soap was clean and fragrant, she poured it into molds to cure for several weeks.

Each week she mixed another batch, changing the fragrance with whatever she could gather in the countryside. She boiled pine needles for their spicy pungency. Consuela brought her mulberries which gave a soft, fruity smell and imparted a lovely color to the soap. Antonio got his hands on a small crate of lemons shipped from the southern California territory. Consuela used the lemons for cooking, then turned over the peels to Linnea to extract the fragrant oils from the skins. Linnea made unscented soap and liquid soap, too, that she poured into glass jars Consuela salvaged from her extended family.

The spring equinox brought anticipation for warm weather and trying out Linnea's first batch of soap. The gentle fragrance that wafted from Linnea's skin and hair teased Antonio's nose and haunted his dreams. He quickly grew to associate the scent of orange and cinnamon with soft, pale skin, fiery hair, and emerald eyes. He found himself fantasizing about stroking that smooth skin to see if it was as silky as he imagined. He wondered if she tasted as delicious as she smelled. He admired her diligence and hard work and creativity with the soaps she created and thought Linnea would be a lovely asset to any household. He delighted in her company, and they shared stories of their childhoods far across the Atlantic Ocean. He added Swedish to his repertoire of languages. Alone in his cot, Antonio groaned with unfulfilled desire and thanked God that Linnea lived in his house.

He did not know if she felt the same.

Preparing to proceed with her plans for commercial success, the young woman wrapped small cakes of soap in colorful bits of cloth and ribbons. She looked forward to selling her products.

Unfortunately, her presence in Antonio's household did not go unnoticed during the months of her residence with the undertaker. Rampant gossip spread rumors about the undertaker's kept woman. The physician let out word that the woman hailed from the Swedish immigrants camped north of town. Merchants who begrudgingly accepted Consuela as their customer because she purchased goods on behalf of the undertaker refused to serve Linnea.

"Your kind ain't welcome here," one merchant sniffed.

"I only deal with respectable ladies," another said as he pointed her toward the door. "Now get out or I'll have you thrown out."

"They won't let me buy anything from them," she complained. "How am I going to persuade them to let me sell my wares to them?"

Consuela had an idea. "Perhaps they will buy from one of my daughters."

She drafted Lucia into dressing in her Sunday best and carrying a basket of prettily packaged soaps to the different merchants to sell. The merchants refused to buy from that young woman, too.

Her presence revealed to the local populace, Linnea saw no point in hiding anymore. She attended Mass with Antonio, and the kindly priest welcomed her. She offered the first batch of her soaps to Consuela's many relatives who thanked her with bright smiles and appreciative sniffs of the fragrant bars. She carried a basket of soaps the long distance to the immigrant camp where the folks there expressed incredulous surprise that she lived, and they welcomed her miraculous return from the dead. However, they could not afford to buy her soaps. They had more than enough to do fending off the Jenkins gang and recovering from those depredations. She gave her soaps away rather than lug them back to Antonio's home. She visited her family's old homestead, the ruined buildings haphazardly rebuilt and now occupied by a family of squatters who ran her off *their* land.

She returned despondent.

She stopped making soap.

"She is sad," Consuela confided in a soft whisper. "She is lonely, Señor Antonio."

"I know," he agreed and glanced at the empty doorway as his housekeeper set a tray with his lunch on the desk. "But I don't know what to do about it. It seems I saved her life only for her to be miserable."

"Did not Father Ramón say that God had a purpose in bringing her to you?" the woman reminded him.

"Yes, but she does not seem to love me." He sighed.

"Perhaps she is afraid to love you."

"What do you mean?"

"Bah! You are a good man, Señor Antonio, but stupid. You treat her as you would a guest or sister."

"Well, I'm certainly not going to force myself upon her."

"Do you let her know your feelings?" the older woman demanded.

He shook his head and said, "If she cares for me, then why does she not say something?"

"*Estupido.* You are all she has. If she says or does anything to upset you, she fears she has no home, no friend, no nothing."

Tony hadn't thought of the situation from Linnea's fragile perspective, but his housekeeper made good sense.

"Linnea, come for a walk with me," Tony said after supper that evening.

"A walk?"

"Yes. We'll get a bit of fresh air and see how the preparations are coming along for the spring festival. It's held the week before Easter this year. Everyone from miles around will come."

"What does everyone do at this festival?" she asked as he took her hand and tucked it into the crook of his arm. He led her outside and they walked along the edge of the muddy road.

"There's music and dancing. After being shut inside all winter, people are mad to get out and sell the handicrafts they made and buy what they didn't make. We'll set up a stall for you, so you can sell your soaps." He paused to smile at her. "They're quite wonderful, you know. They remind me of the Marseille soaps the wealthy used in Italy."

She nodded, thinking about the booth. "I learned from one of the Marseille soap makers."

"Ah! That is why."

"Would you really set up a booth for me? Do you really think that people will buy?"

"Folks from twenty miles around come to this festival. They don't know you or know your history."

"You mean they don't think I'm your whore," she said, every word bitter on her tongue.

He stopped and took her shoulders in his hands to turn her to face him. "Linnea, surely they are not saying such things."

Her trembling lip and the shine of sudden tears informed him otherwise.

"Oh, you poor darling," he whispered and pulled her into his embrace. "We must go to see Father Ramón."

"Why?"

Taking a deep breath, he girded himself for rejection. His teeth gleamed in a brave smile. "Because, my dear Linnea, I have fallen in love with you. Dare I hope that you care for me?"

Eyes wide and shining, she nodded. For the first time, she admitted to the deep, abiding feelings she felt for the man who saved her life and gave her a home. She looked into his warm, brown eyes and found herself smiling. She raised her hand to cup his cheek.

"Dear Antonio, how could you doubt that? I owe everything to you."

"Linnea, I don't want your gratitude."

She flinched at the harsh tone and realized she'd bungled. "But you have my gratitude and more. Everything that I am I would give to you."

"You would consent to being an undertaker's wife?"

She chuckled. "You're the only undertaker who brings people back to life."

He grinned and his arms tightened around her. He whispered, "Only those whom I love."

They parted. Hand in hand, they walked back home.

The next day, Antonio spoke with the priest who expressed his pleasure in uniting the two in holy matrimony. Cletus built a simple booth and bench that he and Billy set up at the spring festival the following week. As promised, folks from miles around descended upon the town. Linnea soon sold out of her wares and found herself inundated with orders for more. Antonio received word that a property had opened in Pine Bluff, a town about twenty miles west and from where most of Linnea's orders had come.

Easter came and went, a holiday filled with prayer and celebration. Linnea, Billy, Cletus, and Antonio spent it with Consuela's extended family. The following week, Antonio and Linnea got married and learned what the word *fiesta* truly meant as Consuela and her relatives celebrated the happy couple late into the night.

Two weeks later, the town of Crescent Hill bemoaned the departure of the most elegant funeral equipage they'd ever seen as the undertaker, his bride, and his staff moved to Pine Bluff where the Swedish immigrant soon built a thriving business making and selling fine soaps and candles and the most distinguished undertaker in the territory conducted the most elegant funerals.

The Rancher's First Love

When a gravely wounded Chinese woman collapses on Clint Cheswick's front porch, he doesn't expect to compete with his half-breed foreman for her affection.

Clint grabbed his shotgun from its customary position by the door and opened it immediately after hearing a thud on the wooden floor of the spacious veranda that wrapped around the house. He listened for a moment and heard nothing. With supreme caution, he flung open the door and leveled the gun, ready to shoot.

Peering into the darkness, he saw nothing. A low moan drew his attention downward to a crumpled heap of bloody fabric and long, dark hair. With a curse, he stashed the shotgun beside the door frame and squatted beside the woman who bled all over his veranda.

"Colt! Matilda!" he shouted. His housekeeper and younger brother rushed to aid him.

"What's up?" Colton asked as he skidded to a stop beside Clint. "Who's that?"

"Lawd have mercy!" Matilda exclaimed, the whites of her eyes stark against coffee colored skin. "Mister Clint, that's a girl what's bleedin' all over my nice, clean floor that I mopped just this afternoon!"

He pressed his fingertips to the back of the woman's left shoulder. She groaned in response.

"She's been shot in the back," he murmured and looked up at his brother. "Colt, help me carry her inside. We've got to take care of her."

"How we gonna do that without killin' her?"

"Get the stretcher from the stable, the one we use when one of the hands is hurt."

"Gotcha," Colton replied. He ran off to do his brother's bidding and returned a few minutes later with the stretcher and the ranch's foreman, an Apache half-breed everyone called Dagger, because he did not deign to give anyone his real name. Clint doubted his real name was a Christian name and ignored the rumors. Dagger was a damned fine foreman.

While Matilda fluttered about like an anxious hen, the men rolled the woman onto a stretcher and carried her into the kitchen where they laid her on the long kitchen table. She groaned and cried in pain, but her eyes never opened. Clint did not see an exit wound on the front of her, which meant the bullet was lodged in her flesh somewhere.

"Matilda, get some clean rags and some water," Clint ordered. "Colt, you see if you can find one of Mama's old nightgowns to put on her."

Colton's eyes bugged. "You gonna strip her, Clint?"

"If I'm gonna clean that wound and dig out that bullet, yeah, I've got to strip her. And I got to find out if she's been hurt anywhere else."

Dagger grunted and placed the flat of his palm against

the woman's ribs beneath her small breasts. He muttered one word: "Strong."

"She'll have to be to survive this," Clint muttered as he pulled a knife from the sheath attached to his belt and began slicing off the first layer of clothing.

"Mister Clint!" Matilda squawked in outrage. "You got no bidness disrobing a woman." She held out her broad palm. "Give me that knife and *you* go fetch that water." She turned to Dagger and ordered, "And *you* put the water on t'boil."

The two men obeyed, trying but not succeeding in averting their eyes as the housekeeper peeled strips of fabric from smooth, golden flesh.

"Oh, Lord-a-mercy," the housekeeper muttered as her ministrations revealed deep, dark bruising. "Someone done beat this girl near unto death."

"Who'd do such a thing?" Colton asked, peeking through the kitchen door.

"Mister Colton, y'all's too young to see such things. Get yo' skinny white backside upstairs and back to bed."

"Yessum," Colton replied. He placed the old, folded nightgown on a countertop and backed away from the door, reluctantly obedient. He knew that Matilda still believed him young enough to endure a whipping and would have no hesitation in cutting off a willow switch to use on his backside. Ever since Mama got sick and passed away, Matilda had assumed that role, and she took no guff from "her" boys—or any of the men on the ranch.

"Colt, why don't you saddle Lightning and head to Doc Branson's? Tell him we got an emergency here."

"Will do, Clint!" the sixteen-year old boy replied and rushed out the door.

"Now why'd you do that, Mister Clint?"

"Matilda, we're gonna need a doctor. I'm liable to hurt this poor woman further by trying to dig the slug out of her."

She harrumphed as they flipped the woman over to expose her back. She cut away the layers of blood-soaked fabric and tilted her head. She dipped a rag into a bowl of water, wrung it out, and dabbed at the wound.

"Inch or so to the right or down and she'd be dead," Matilda said.

The woman keened as pain blossomed anew.

"Hold her down, Mister Clint. Dagger, you, too."

Male hands, rough and strong from hard, manual labor, anchored the woman down as Matilda cleaned the wound with ruthless efficiency. The woman cried out and struggled against the onslaught of new pain. Clint clenched his jaws, every part of him rebelling against any action that caused the woman any additional pain. He winced at the deep bruising that wrapped around her right side to her lower back.

"My God," he said. "As badly as she's been beaten, shooting her was just overkill."

"Clint! Clint! Doc's here!" Colton's shout rang through the house.

"Back in the kitchen, Doc!" Clint called out.

Fussing with his spectacles, Dr. Branson carried his medical bag into the kitchen and stopped to gape at the bruised and bloody woman on Matilda's usually spotless table.

"Bullet's lodged somewhere in the back of her left shoulder, Doc," Clint explained as Matilda dabbed at the bleeding wound.

"Who is she?" Dr. Branson inquired as he pulled out a small pair of forceps.

"Don't know."

"She ain't white."

"She's one o' them China girls," Matilda said. "Her kin's prolly workin' on railroad construction." She fingered the cheap satin skirt. "Looks like she be a workin' girl."

"Way she's been beaten, I'd say she didn't want to be a

'workin' girl,'" Clint commented.

Dagger simply grunted.

"You men hold her down. I'm gonna dig for that slug," the doctor said and brandished his weapon of choice.

Clint and Dagger renewed their grips on the unknown woman's torso and legs. The doctor plunged the forceps into her flesh and the woman's eyes opened wide as she screamed and arched and thrashed to get away from the pain as he dug around inside her wound. He pulled back and dropped a shard of bloody bone on the table.

"Clean her up, Matilda, I can't see nothing," the doctor ordered.

Matilda shot the doctor a sharp glance, pressed full lips together in a thin line, and obeyed. When the wound was more or less clear again, the doctor went fishing a second time. The woman finally grunted and blacked out. The other people in the room heaved a collective sigh of relief. The doctor dug out another shard of bone and dropped it on the tabletop. Twice more he dug into the wound and finally extracted a misshapen slug.

After Matilda cleaned the wound and poured a good measure of her employer's grain whiskey over it, the physician stitched it and wrapped a bandage over it.

"She'll likely succumb to fever," he said and pulled out a small jar of white powder. "This is salicylic acid. Mix a small spoonful in water four times daily and make her drink it. It will help with the pain and inflammation."

As he reached into his bag, he said, "It's extremely bitter, so don't be shy about stirring in some honey, or maple syrup if you have it." He pulled out another small bottle. "And this is laudanum. Just a few drops as needed to keep her sedated and to dull the pain for at least three days."

He handed the glass containers to Matilda. "Since you're the only female on the premises, I assume you'll be the one to care for the patient's needs?"

Matilda nodded.

The doctor closed his bag and wiped his hands on a clean rag. "Then my work here is done for tonight. I'll stop by in a day or two to check on her."

Clint followed the man out of the kitchen to pay him for his time and trouble.

"Clint, those Chinamen are trouble," the doctor warned. "They're unclean pagans."

Clint sighed, since he'd heard much the same about Dagger. "Thanks, Doc. But all I see is a woman who's been badly hurt."

The doctor shrugged, accepted the rancher's money, and headed out the door to return to his bed.

"Is she all right?" Colton whispered from the front parlor as Clint turned to walk back to the kitchen.

"She's not out of the woods yet, but I think she's got a fighting chance," he replied.

"She's strong," Dagger reiterated.

"She's kind of purty, real delicate looking," the rancher's young brother remarked.

"That she is," Clint agreed. "You wanna help Dagger and me get her upstairs?"

"Where you gonna put her?"

"Your room."

"My room!"

"Yeah, you can take my bed and I'll move into Ma and Pa's room."

"How come you get the big bedroom?"

"'Cause I'm the oldest and the boss."

Colton pouted, but he followed his brother into the kitchen nonetheless.

Matilda shooed the men out of her kitchen and did her best to clean the small, fine-boned woman, stripping her naked and pulling on the old nightgown over the frail, bruised body. She tossed the bloodied rags into the kitchen fire.

"We'll take good care o' ya," the woman murmured to

the unconscious woman.

At her word, Clint and Colton returned. Clint scooped the woman into his arms where she rested limp as a wet dishrag. Colton raced upstairs to hold open the bedroom door and turn down the covers on his narrow bed. He watched as his brother set her down and then drew the blankets over her.

"You get on to bed, Colton. You got school tomorrow."

"Ah, Clint, do I gotta?"

"Yes. You know Mama wanted one of us to get a good education. Since I'm stuck here runnin' the ranch, that's you."

"But what if I don't wanna go to some fancy college back east?"

"Don't matter. It's what Mama wanted and we ain't gonna disappoint her."

"It ain't fair."

"You think I wanted to run this ranch before I was even eighteen?" Clint shot back. "Mama and Pa, too, wanted one of us to have opportunities beyond runnin' cattle and eatin' dust. You'll go to college and become a fancy doctor or lawyer or some such and make our parents proud."

Colton shook his head and trudged toward his brother's room, muttering under his breath, "They're dead, I'm not."

Clinton pulled a straight-backed chair near the bed and sat down to watch over his patient.

"I sure hope you can tell me what the hell happened to you, girl," he whispered.

A few hours later, Matilda relieved him. Grateful for the reprieve, he went to bed thinking as he lay down that the pillowcase and sheets still smelled somewhat of his father's shaving soap and his mother's favorite lemon verbena scent, even though his parents had been dead for almost ten years.

The next morning, their patient still lay unconscious,

but she burned with fever. Clint sent his brother off to school and enlisted Matilda's kitchen maid to help with tending the unknown woman. He had work to do that didn't wait upon the whims of an uninvited guest.

Two more days passed before the woman's fever broke and she opened her eyes. Matilda made good use of her employer's mother's nightgowns and diligently tended the young woman.

"It don' matta that you yellow and me black," she whispered in the patois of her youth. "We both women unner da skin, and a woman need a little comfort."

"Wh—where am I?" the Chinese woman whispered, her words heavily accented, but in clear English.

"Lord-a-mercy, you *do* speak a civilized tongue," Matilda exclaimed with a smile, strong white teeth brilliant against her dark skin. "Young lady, you's at the Cheswick Ranch. Clinton Cheswick is master here."

The dark slanted eyes blinked.

Matilda remembered the drugs left by the doctor and administered them, despite the young woman trying to refuse to take them. With the expediency of a woman who'd had to wrestle young boys into doing what they didn't want to do, she prevailed against the weakened patient's defiance.

"I know it taste bad, girl, but you gots to take it. Doctor says so."

A few more days passed with Clint, Colton, and Dagger briefly popping in for quick visits. The doctor returned to check on her, too, poking none too gently at the wound and making her hiss with pain.

"I guess Chinamen feel discomfort, too," the doctor muttered. "Rather like animals, they are."

He returned home to begin writing a paper on the treatment of Chinamen and how it differed from the treatment of white folk. He fantasized about the accolades his insights would earn from his learned peers. Others had written treatises on the differences and similarities between those of lowly African descent and their superiors of European descent, but he knew of no scholars who had researched the differences between the barbaric Asians from China and white folks. Why, his paper would be groundbreaking!

"D'you think Doc's right?" Colton asked his brother at supper.

Dagger took a biscuit from a basket and bit into it, chewing without comment.

"About what?" Clint prompted.

"That Chinamen, like black folks, is only three-fifths human and the rest animal?"

Dagger snorted, nostrils flaring.

"You wanna tell Matilda she ain't a real human being?" Clint challenged the boy, eyes glinting.

Colton turned pale at the thought. "No, sir."

"Right. That girl's just as human as you, me, Dagger, and Matilda. What matters is what's inside, not what color God made 'em."

Dagger snorted again, but more softly. Then he grunted.

Clint looked at him. "You wanna check on her?"

The half-breed nodded, a single dip of his chin.

"Go ahead. She might like to see a face that ain't one of ours."

Dagger nodded again and shoved himself away from the table.

"That man ain't got no manners," Matilda complained as she bustled into the dining room to set down plates laden with slices of fruit pie.

"Where'd you find apples, Matilda?" Colton asked after shoveling a forkful into his mouth.

"Don't chew with your mouth open, boy," the woman chided. "And that ain't apple, it's green pumpkin." She grinned at him and took a bite. After swallowing, she added, "Tastes good, don't it?"

"Yessum."

"Matilda, I swear you could make dirt taste good," Clint praised. "Y'all mind if I take a bit to our guest?"

"You go right ahead, young man. Girl ain't got enough appetite to keep a bird alive."

Clint nodded and took the plate intended for Dagger upstairs, snagging a fork and napkin on the way. Colton followed soon after with a glass of milk squeezed from the cow that morning.

The two men paused and gaped at the sight of the fierce half-breed holding the patient's delicate hand as he murmured to her.

"Dagger?" Colton blurted in amazement. He'd never seen the foreman act in such a tender manner, unless he was ministering to a sick or injured horse.

"We brought pie," Clint said, feeling awkward.

The woman looked at him, her expression curious.

"Pie," he repeated in a louder tone and mimed eating with exaggerated gestures. The woman nodded and whispered something that made the corner of Dagger's mouth twitch in amusement. That small twitch on Dagger's face equaled uncontrolled laughter in any other man. In all his twenty-six years, Clint had never seen another man so self-contained as his foreman.

With grave grace, the woman took the plate in weak hands. Colton set the glass of milk on the small bedside table. She ate the offering, first with a tentative taste, then with cautious enthusiasm. She treated the milk the same way.

"Don't they have cows in China?" Colton asked under his breath.

"I dunno."

"She does not trust white men," Dagger said in a low tone.

"She speaks English?" Clinton asked, eyebrows raised.

"Some." Dagger glance at her then looked back at the

Cheswick men. "White men stole her from her family."

"And her family? Where are they?"

"Dead." A fierce light flared in the man's dark eyes. "From what she said, they died at the hands of my father's people."

"Huh?"

"A raid," Dagger said succinctly. "They worked on the railroad passing through Apache territory. My father's people attacked, killed the railroad workers. White soldiers then attacked my father's people. They slaughtered the surviving Chinamen and sold the women to brothels." He glanced at her. "She belongs to my people, a prize of battle."

"If your people killed hers, then why would she trust you and not us?" Clint asked.

"Death in battle is honorable," came the laconic answer.

"Well, I think we've shown her that not all white men are dishonorable," Colton said.

"She is grateful for your kindness."

Clint sighed. "Would you tell her it's all right to talk to us? We ain't gonna hurt her."

Dagger nodded. He returned to the woman's bedside and spoke to her in low tones. After a moment, he turned back to his employer. "She will answer your questions."

"Thanks, Dagger," Clint said in clear dismissal. Really, the foreman was running awfully tame in the Cheswick household.

Clint took the chair the half-breed had abandoned and made himself comfortable. He looked at the small, delicate woman lying in his brother's narrow bed. She returned his gaze with an inscrutable, steady look that discomfited him.

"Um ... my name's Clint, Clint Cheswick."

Her head moved in a small nod. She replied in a soft voice no louder than a whisper, "Thank you. You help me."

He found her accent intriguing; however, she still looked tired and drawn, so he decided not to waste time on chit chat. "Can you tell me what happened to you?"

The golden skin over her cheekbones darkened and he realized she was blushing. However, he said nothing; he simply waited for her to answer.

"I—I no want ... to ... to ..." She sighed and looked away in shame. "They beat me ... I say no ... I run." She took a breath. "He shoot me. I still run ... see you big house ... think, get help."

Speaking slowly and taking care to enunciate, Clint said, "Dagger says your pa and brother were working on the railroad going into Santa Fe."

She nodded.

"Those tracks go right through Apache territory."

She blinked.

"Dagger's pa is Apache. He says that Apaches attacked the railroad."

She blinked again. Apparently, he told her nothing she did not already know. However, her lack of surprise at least confirmed that Dagger had informed him correctly.

"Dagger also said that soldiers rode in to fight the Apaches, but they killed everyone who wasn't a woman or child."

She nodded, her face tightening. The small muscle at the base of her jaw bulged as she clenched her teeth.

He sighed, knowing where the story went. "I got no pull with the U.S. cavalry, but I can't excuse what they did to innocent people." He set his hand over hers. It fluttered beneath his palm like a trapped butterfly. "All I can say is you're safe here."

"Thank you."

"Is there anything I can get for you?"

"Water? Soap?"

"You want to wash?" he asked.

Her cheeks darkened with another blush, but she nodded to confirm his guess. Rising, he rubbed his palms on his thighs. "I'll have Matilda fill a bath for you. There ...

there ain't no other women here but you and her."

With his words, he felt the burn of his own blush, especially as his mind's eye recalled the smooth slope of her firm, golden flesh laid bare on the kitchen table. Except for the rare trip into town, he had no interaction with women other than his housekeeper. The very idea of an intimate relationship with Matilda—who had changed his diapers—made him cringe.

He excused himself and headed downstairs to risk his life interrupting the housekeeper in the middle of preparing lunch for the hands. Glowering at him, she raised her cleaver.

"Dear Lawd, you tell that brother o' yourn to fill the hip bath. I'll get the girl after lunch. That means someone else'll have to tidy up after and wash them dishes."

"I'll get some volunteers," he promised with the intention of "volunteering" whoever annoyed him the most at the midday meal.

"Don't you think you c'n dump that girl on me, Mister Clint," the older woman threatened, waving that cleaver. "I got no time to babysit a grown woman."

"Perhaps she can do some mending or something like that," he suggested.

"Mebbe she can." The dark eyes blinked. "You need ta fetch her somewhat to wear. Your ma's dresses is too big for a bitty little thing like her."

"The only thing that might fit her are Colton's old hand-me-downs," Clint pointed out.

Matilda grunted and brought the cleaver down, severing the chicken carcass in one deft stroke.

"It wouldn't be proper for her to wear Colt's old clothes," Clint protested.

"It ain't proper for her to be sleeping in your brother's bed, neither," the housekeeper retorted. "Seems to me like we was beyond propriety. Them snooty old biddies in town won't know and wouldn't care none about the likes of her if they did."

Clint said nothing, knowing that Matilda's disgust of those same "snooty old biddies" arose from their treatment of her. He sighed at the strange limits of the Christian virtues people professed but did not extend to those they deemed inferior.

"I got to head into town tomorrow. If I buy some cloth, would you sew it into something for … for her to wear?" Clint rubbed his neck, realizing that he did not yet know the woman's name. Idly, he wondered if he could even pronounce it. Dagger had attempted to teach him some useful Apache phrases, but his clumsy tongue simply could not manage the complicated language. Sometimes, he overheard Matilda mutter to herself in the tribal language she'd learned from her mother and the gibberish sounded awfully complex to him, not at all clear like English.

If folks could master those languages, and English, why did it follow that they were less than fully human? The discrepancy puzzled him.

"I can do that. She'll need a hat, too," Matilda answered him as she expertly separated four chickens into pieces with that wickedly sharp cleaver. "Every respectable woman needs a hat."

"You're sure she's respectable?" Clint quipped.

Matilda raised her head and the cleaver and glared at him. His grin disappeared.

"That girl got herself beat and shot 'cause she wouldn't shame herself, you hear me, boy? Don't you besmirch her character."

Clint's face flushed red with shame. "No, ma'am."

Matilda nodded. "Good. Now git."

He got.

With two bolts of cloth, Matilda added to her duties by sewing two simple dresses for the Cheswicks' guest, who finally gave them her name: Yu-xing. Dagger continued to visit every day, two, three, or even four times a day. The

Chinese girl and the half-breed spoke softly to each other, the latter glowering at anyone who dared interrupt them. Clinton found himself annoyed at what he saw as the foreman hogging Yu-xing's attention.

Yu-xing. He rolled the name over his tongue and wondered what it meant, for surely it meant something in the sing-song language that he overheard her use when she muttered to herself. He wondered if muttering aloud to oneself was something women in general did and wished he could remember if his mother had indulged in the same habit. When asked, Colton couldn't remember either. He didn't dare ask Matilda.

Nearly four weeks after she collapsed on his doorstep, Yu-xing joined the family and ranch hands for supper. Clinton sternly reminded the hands to mind their manners and speech. Dagger's glittering black eyes and the suggestive slide of his thumb along the sheath of the big knife he always wore enforced the boss' admonition. Eager to escort their guest, Colton seated Yu-xing in the chair between him and Dagger at Clint's right hand. After loading the table with bowls and platters and baskets filled with food, Matilda took her place at Clint's left hand, a position of honor that none of the hands dared protest. As was customary, Matilda led the group in saying grace over their meal.

On their best behavior, the ranch hands kept their conversation civil and at a slightly lower volume than normal.

"Git y'all's elbows off the table, boy," Matilda hissed at Colton, who blushed and obeyed.

Clint found his gaze straying more often than not to Yu-xing, admiring the shining raven swoop of her hair into a simple coil at the base of her skull. The deep red of the cotton fabric she wore flattered her golden complexion. Only the faint mottling of fading bruises showed above the modest neckline.

Damn, she's pretty!

But she apparently had eyes for the half-breed.

Clint watched them interact. Dagger certainly didn't cater to her like Colton did or treat her as invalid. The foreman watched her closely though, silently assisting only when and where she seemed to need it. He noticed they seldom spoke to each other. A casual observer might have said the Chinese woman and the half breed man mostly ignored each other.

Jealous, Clint paid close attention. Yu-xing reserved her small smiles for the half-breed.

I want those smiles!

Clint seethed with resentment. Why should Dagger get Yu-xing's favor when it was he, the elder Cheswick, who had summoned the doctor and provided her with medicine, food, shelter, and clothing. Damn it, she owed him!

As though sensing his employer's ire, Dagger locked his inscrutable, glittering eyes with Clint's. The half-breed's nostrils flared in silent challenge. The man's haughty features seemed to invite confrontation as though to say, "If you can beat me, then you'll be worthy of her."

Clint lowered his eyes, breaking the connection and backing down from the challenge. He'd seen Dagger fight. Every time he hired a new hand who then objected to being bossed by a half-breed—which was nearly all of them— Dagger challenged them to a fight and then soundly beat the hell out of them. The tactic worked and no one gave Dagger any guff.

The more Clint thought about it, the more he thought that Dagger treated nothing as gently and with such acute awareness as he did Yu-xing and his three horses.

She's more than a horse; she's a woman.

He sighed as he watched them.

"What's got your britches twisted?" Colton hissed at him.

"What?"

"You're looking at Yu-xing and Dagger like you want to

hurt them."

"I don't want to hurt them."

Colton's eyes widened with sudden knowledge and he crowed, "You're jealous!"

"Keep your voice down, Colt."

"Well, she's real pretty, but she ain't like us, Clint."

Clint stared at his brother.

"She ain't like us," the boy repeated. "Folks in town wouldn't never accept her, no more'n if you married Matilda."

Clint sighed, because his little brother was right.

The boy grinned. "'Sides, I hear Doc Branson's girl is old enough for courtin'."

"And where did you hear that?"

"Doc Branson. He made sure to tell me that Lizzie-Beth is turnin' eighteen next month."

"You seen her?"

"Last year when I went to town with Matilda. Saw her in the mercantile. She was pretty. Yeller hair. Blue dress." Colton tilted his head and with the startling perspicacity of youth asked, "You feelin' lonely?"

"Ma and Pa were married at my age," Clint replied and cast one more longing glance at Yu-xing. "They loved each other so much. I want that, too."

"Don't be wantin' what you can't have," Colton whispered in empathy, darting a glance at the Yu-xing. "Mebbe you'll like Lizzie-Beth Branson."

"I suppose I'd best find out. If I make a move on the woman Dagger wants, he'll slaughter me."

"Ain't no woman worth that."

Resigning himself to leaving the current love of his life to his foreman, he found himself looking forward to seeing what eligible young ladies the town had to offer.

Looking around the table as he ate, he caught Dagger's gaze again. The man's hard black eyes seemed to radiate satisfaction that the younger man finally understood and accepted the reality that the pretty woman in his household was not meant for him. Clint wondered how Dagger knew that, but he did not question the man's uncanny perception. His gaze moved to Yu-xing and she met his eyes with her own. In her gaze, he saw gratitude and a cautious friendship. Then she blinked and severed the fleeting connection.

When the meal ended, Clint rose from the table and walked to his foreman.

"You'll marry her," he insisted in a low voice so as not to be overheard.

"I'll say the white man's words," the half-breed replied.

"You hurt her and I'll kill you."

"She is the moon and stars to my sun, the earth to my rain," Dagger said. He blinked slowly, then added, "She knows my name."

Clint strained not to gape. Dagger told *no one* his name. After a moment, he gathered his composure and said, "I guess we'd best build you a house, 'cause Yu-xing won't want to live in the bunkhouse."

Dagger favored him with the first smile he'd ever seen from the man. "No, the bunkhouse isn't a good place for children."

Clint bristled. "You didn't!"

Dagger's amusement vanished. "I would not dishonor my wife."

Yu-xing walked to Dagger's side and stood quietly. Clint watched as the man reached for her hand and clasped it in his own. Something dark and lethal seemed to ease in the foreman's expression and Clint realized he had let loose an exhalation of relief. Something about that small woman calmed the deadly rage that lived inside the half-breed.

"You love her," he whispered.

Dagger replied with a tiny nod.

Clint looked at Yu-xing and asked, "Do you love him?"

"*Shi,*" she replied with a nod, looking more confident

and brave than he'd ever seen her. Her own dark eyes seemed to sparkle with joy and pride. "Yes, he is fierce and has much honor. I no fear with him."

And that, he supposed, said it all.

Yu-xing's words cut free any lingering romantic thoughts Clint entertained concerning her. That hurt. He thought again about a pretty girl with golden hair and bright blue eyes that sparkled in the sun. He'd best invite the Branson family over for supper soon, before the young bucks in town learned she was ready to be married off.

Turning his attention back to his foreman and his guest, the young rancher said, "I'll hire a crew to build you a house out by the creek. It'll be my wedding gift to y'all."

"Thank you," the lovers replied.

Clint took his leave and headed back to the house. Matilda waylaid him.

"That's a good thing you done, Mister Clint."

He gave her a bittersweet smile. "I could have loved her, too."

She patted his arm in commiseration. She agreed; he could have loved the mysterious young woman and been miserable for it. He needed a simple girl with simple expectations who would fit in with the other ranchers' wives. "I heard that Doc Branson's girl, Lizzie-Beth, is ready fer courtin'."

"Yeah, I heard the same thing."

"There's a dance bein' held first Saturday next month. You go there and have fun. I'll ride herd on young Colt."

His smile eased. "You're good to me, Matilda."

She smiled at him, white teeth brilliant against coffee colored skin. "You's the son of my heart and I wants ta see y'all happy."

Ranch owner Clinton Cheswick hugged his housekeeper and basked in the warmth of her affection. He eventually would have love, marriage, and a family—although not with Lizzie-Beth Branson—but, even in his dotage, he never forgot the delicate, resilient, exotic woman who had first captured his heart without even trying. Her black-haired, copper-skinned children who spoke three languages—Chinese, Apache, and English—provided him with a constant reminder.

Thank you!

Thank you for reading *Satin Boots*. I hope you enjoyed reading this collection of sweet, short romances as much as I did writing it.

Authors depend greatly upon reader reviews. Please leave your review on Amazon. If you wish to contact me directly with comments related to this or any other of my books, send a message to me through the contact page on the Hen House Publishing website: https://henhousepub-lishing.com.

About the Author

Holly Bargo is a pseudonym, but really did exist as a temperamental Appaloosa mare fondly remembered for protecting toddler children and crushing a pager. The author and her husband live on a hobby farm in southwest Ohio where they take care of a menagerie of four-legged beasties. Holly works full-time as a freelance writer, ghost-writer, editor.

The author and her husband have two children, both grown. Now officially rulers of an empty nest, they contemplate retirement off the farm.

Holly enjoys engaging with readers and maintains a blog on her website: https://www.henhousepublishing. com/blog.html. To send a message to Holly Bargo, use the contact form on the Hen House Publishing website: https://www.henhousepublishing.com/contact.html.

More Books by Holly Bargo

All titles listed below are available for purchase from Amazon, except where noted with an asterisk. Check my Amazon author page: https://www.amazon.com/Holly-Bargo/e/B00JRK6VGQ. All books within each series are written as complete, standalone novels. For my readers' peace of mind and my own, I don't write cliffhangers.

Immortal Shifters Series

The Barbary Lion*
Tiger in the Snow
Bear of the Midnight Sun
The Eagle at Dawn

Tree of Life Series

Rowan
Cassia
Willow

Twin Moons Saga

Daughter of the Twin Moons
Daughter of the Deepwood
Daughter of the Dark Moon

Russian Love Series

Russian Lullaby
Russian Gold
Russian Dawn
Russian Pride

Other Novels

The Mighty Finn
Pure Iron
Ulfbehrt's Legacy
The Diamond Gate
The Dragon Wore a Kilt
The Falcon of Imenotash
Triple Burn

Collaborative Work

Six Shots Each Gun: 12 Tales of the Old West
written in collaboration with Russ Towne

Short Stories

By Water Reborn
Skeins of Gold: Rumpelstiltskin Retold